HOG-TIED

Jake Willem and his son Jess, have settled in the Grip Basin. But rancher Hiram Otto Galt and his foreman, Roach Tolman, control the local law — they take what they want and shoot dissenters. Rosie Post inflames tensions further by taking over the Catkin ranch . . . Galt has doubts over what he's become responsible for and there are others who, feeling the same, are drawn into a deadly triangle of opposition. Entrenched camps who've decided there's no way out other than the trading of bullets . . .

Books by Abe Dancer
in the Linford Western Library:

DEATH SONG

ABE DANCER

HOG-TIED

Complete and Unabridged

LINFORD
Leicester

First published in Great Britain in 2005 by
Robert Hale Limited
London

First Linford Edition
published 2006
by arrangement with
Robert Hale Limited
London

British Library CIP Data

Dancer, Abe
    Hog-tied.—Large print ed.—
    Linford western library
    1. Western stories
    2. Large type books
    I. Title
    823.9′2 [F]

    ISBN 1–84617–281–0

Published by
F. A. Thorpe (Publishing)
Anstey, Leicestershire

Set by Words & Graphics Ltd.
Anstey, Leicestershire
Printed and bound in Great Britain by
T. J. International Ltd., Padstow, Cornwall

1

Grip Basin

Just after dawn, the Willems crossed the Wyoming border. At midday, they forded the Cheyenne River. When they arrived in Bullhead, it was under the velvety grey of first dark. Jake was mounted on his bay stallion. Behind him, holding the lines of a short freighter sat his son Jess.

They didn't stop; they walked straight through the town, past weather-scoured buildings where early lights smouldered through open doorways and dusty windows. A few townsfolk watched uncaringly from the board-walks, one or two stayed until both men were out the other side.

After a few minutes, Jake dropped back to the side of the wagon. 'For the changes made, it could've been yesterday I rode through here,' he said. He had a quick glance over his shoulder. 'Maybe it's for the best though. If not, we'd've been robbed o' that place of ours long ago.'

Jess stared into the distance. 'It sure looks an' smells like the sweet land that Gramps was always jawin' about.'

A smile creased Jake's weatherbeaten features. 'Yeah, but let's not forget this Galt feller. He's some sort o' deputy to the Rapid City sheriff — a regulator, some say. He's had a hold on the land hereabouts for nearly a decade, an' don't take much to welcomin' strangers.'

'About time he let go then. Land's supposed to provide for the lame an' the lazy. An' right now, you're lookin' like at least one of 'em.' Jess grinned, peered into the approaching darkness. 'Maybe this is him,' he said.

Jake wasn't possessed of his son's enthusiasm for risk. He watched keenly as the rider drew close enough to run his eyes over the wagon and the mule team. He noticed fancy trappings, the gleam of a nickled Colt.

'Looks like you two are totin' more'n corn,' the man observed. 'You'll be needin' to see Hiram Galt, if you're puttin' down in these parts. He controls just about everythin' in the basin . . . everythin' except me, that is.'

Jess hitched the lines. 'Some sort o' local wild man, are you?' he asked, with a twist of smile.

'There's some would say that. I'm Roach Tolman . . . HOG ranch foreman.'

Tolman turned his attention to Jake's horse, missed the chary glance the two men exchanged. He tipped his sharp-brimmed hat up from his forehead. 'That's a fine-lookin' blood you're ridin'. Too fine for hay shakin'. If you want a fair price for him, I'll give it to you.'

Jake looked from Tolman to Jess, back to Tolman. 'It pleases me to know that, Tolman. But the horse ain't up for sale,' he said evenly. Then he leaned forward and gently tugged the stallion's dark mane.

A flash of irritation showed suddenly in Tolman's face. 'This horse I'm ridin' an' fifty dollars on top. That's the best offer you'll get anywhere in these parts.'

Jake cursed patiently. 'I don't care if it's the best offer east *an'* west o' the Missouri. I just told you, my horse ain't for sale.'

'It *is*, mister. We just ain't hit on a price,' Tolman persisted.

Jake shook his head as he caught the insolence in Tolman's voice. He pressed the palm of his hand against the grip of his Colt, nudged the bay forward. 'I just got to see how much horse turd you got stuffed in your ears,' he rasped.

Tolman backed his horse off a couple of paces. 'Whatever piece o' home ground you're after, I'm wagerin' it'll support nothin' more'n canker worms,' he sneered.

Jess clicked the mules forward. 'Me an' my pa got good land along the Oglala Creek. It's filed an' paid for, so we won't be seein' any goddamn grubs, an' that includes you an' Hiram Galt,' he yelled at Tolman. 'Now, move aside, wild man, or I'll be runnin' you down.'

The blood pulsed fast in Roach Tolman. Restraint wasn't part of his make-up, but Jake had anticipated the man's reaction. He heeled the bay's flanks as Tolman raised the whip he carried in his left hand.

The stallion lunged, his muscled shoulder piling into Tolman's sorrel. The animal shivered with the impact and Tolman was shaken. He clutched at the saddle horn, stared into a long-barrelled six-gun.

'You ain't layin' that quirt,' Jake snapped. 'I'll break open your ugly great head first.' Jake turned the Colt grip forward, ran the barrel along his forearm. 'Me an' my boy here had hoped to be at the creek before mornin', so you *will* be movin' aside.' With that, he slammed the frame of the gun against the sorrel's rump.

'I think I'm fallin' in love with Grip

Basin, Pa. There ain't been a dull moment since we got here,' Jess chuckled as Tolman took to his enraged flight.

'Yeah, let's move on. Else we'll be breakfastin' on lead,' Jake said, with feigned amusement.

2

Bullhead Kill

Before the first wisps of frost touched the basin, Jake and Jess Willem had shaped and built a snug log cabin. It was nestled among late golden rod and larkspur and they named it Two Jays. They worked through the harsh winter, learned to understand and value the land and their new home. In the basin, streams ran wild with melt water and pastures turned lush green. The cherry trees around Bullhead's town square were carrying blossom when Rosie Post arrived.

Like Jake Willem, nobody knew where she'd come from, only that she came in on the Deadwood coach. Holding the hand of a little boy, she stood outside of the stage office. The pair were overawed by the immensity and colour of the Dakota sunset, were oblivious to the interest their arrival was causing.

Rosie Post's eyes were grey, and her hair was ebony. Her dark complexion was well suited to Bullhead's unforgiving weather. It was a while before she realized she was being stared at, before she met the eyes of enquiring bystanders. For a while she matched their gaze, then she tugged at the collar of the boy's coat.

Until the incoming mail was sorted, Jake talked with Bill Quarry, who was the owner of the Twist Wind Hotel. When Rosie Post walked in he turned his head and tipped his hat. Their eyes met as she stood the child in front of her, and Jake smiled, nodded a welcome.

Without a word the lady stepped across the reception area to sign the register. As she wrote, Roach Tolman pushed open the front door of the hotel. He stopped and fixed his eyes on Rosie.

'It's quiet at the moment, Mrs Post. I trust you find the front rooms agreeable,' Quarry said, as the lady handed him back the pen.

'Thank you, I'm sure I will,' she said, 'but I'm *Miss* Post. And this is my nephew Tad Raster.'

Quarry nodded at the child. 'Yes, ma'am . . . Tad Raster,' he echoed. He took a key from the desk and, presuming the lady's luggage to be on the sidewalk, walked towards the door.

As Roach Tolman moved aside, Jake caught the expression on his face. It was similar to the look that he'd affected when he saw Jake's blood bay. The HOG foreman turned suddenly and left the hotel without noticing Jake.

Jake delayed his own leaving for a few minutes, then he drove the mule freighter to the livery to get them night stabled. Later, when he, too, signed in at the Twist Wind, he read the name above his own signature.

'Rosemary Post. Pierre.'

It was mealtime when Rosemary Post showed again. She had a word with Quarry, asked for a tray of food to take to her room. She waited by the register desk, then thanked the girl who brought out the food. As she approached the stairs, Roach Tolman rose from his chair at the dining-table.

'I'll help you with that, ma'am,' he said. 'Don't want no spillages.'

Rosie Post looked at him unsmiling. 'It's a platter of cold cuts . . . I'll get by, thank you,' she said.

Tolman stared around him foolishly as sniggers sounded from the table.

'He'll get over it. Won't seem so bad after he's drunk the White Glass dry,' Jake said unconcernedly, as Tolman skipped his peach pie.

★　★　★

Jake was standing on the veranda, building a smoke, when the HOG foreman appeared the following morning. The man's eyes were red-rimmed

10

and watery, the upshot of his night in the saloon.

When he saw Jake, a scowl creased his raw features. 'You goin' to sell me that bay?' he grated.

For months, the question had been repeated by Tolman. On occasion, it stirred a response from Jake.

'You really are a tiresome son-of-a-bitch, Tolman,' he retorted. 'I'll be givin' it to a half-bake before sellin' to you,' Jake retorted.

Tolman sniffed, spat into the street. 'I usually get what I want, Willem.'

'Yeah. Maybe that is the way you'll get it.' Jake lit his cigarette, flipped the spent match at Tolman's feet.

'You're goin' to get burned, feller,' the foreman sniped, his voice parched and whiskey stale.

'You're never less than a full laugh, Tolman. I'll give you that,' Jake goaded.

For a moment Tolman stared at Jake, puzzled. Then the appearance of Rosie Post on the sidewalk stopped a further threat, and his colour improved.

Miss Post was holding her young nephew's hand. Jake touched the brim of his hat and stepped aside. From the street, Tolman coughed self-consciously, held up an acknowledging hand.

As the young lady approached the corner of the hotel, old Tom Owers stepped unsteadily from the narrow alleyway that ran alongside. Looking up and seeing someone he was about to bump into, he stumbled. Rosie Post flinched and, gripping the child, she withdrew a step. But Owers was still cut with a night's rough drinking and he made no obvious effort to avoid her. Instead, he held out dirt-grimed fingers that touched her arm.

It was an instinctive and innocent act, but to Roach Tolman it was an opportunity to get his name on Rosie Post's slate. He rushed at Owers, and before anyone could follow what was happening, he'd seized the old man and was slapping at his small, whiskered face. 'You crazy old rummy,' he ranted.

'This'll teach you to keep your hands to yourself.'

Owers staggered backward. He buckled, but stayed on his feet. His face reddened and a dribble of blood appeared from a cracked lip.

'Please, no. It was nothing. Stop it!' the lady protested, holding the boy close to her side.

But it had little effect. There was only one thing in Owers' bewildered mind. He was being pushed around, slapped into shame. Muttering uncleanly, he reached for the loose belt of his trousers, dragged at an old belt pistol.

Roach Tolman wasn't much affected by the protest, either. And the early light glinted on his Colt as he pulled the trigger.

Owers was still tugging stubbornly at his gun as Tolman's bullet hit him. With a shattered chest he crumpled, fell without a further sound into the hard-packed soil. Rosie Post was struck with disgust as she stared at the feeble body. Jake knew he'd witnessed a cruel killing, knew that Tom Owers was one of Bullhead's most harmless characters. The oldster was a drunk, the gun he carried was nothing more than a rusting relic.

At the sound of the gunshot, a group of men hurried along the street. One of them kneeled and extracted the pistol from Owers' lifeless grasp. He worked at the stiff action and ejected the empty cylinder, held it up for all to see.

Tolman's face drained as he realized the implication. 'He wasn't haulin' up his goddamn pants. How was I to know the gun weren't loaded?' he bristled.

Jake was watching Rosie Post. Her nephew was staring up at the confusion and noise, and she picked him up.

Before anyone had time to respond to the shooting, a small, bowed woman came shuffling from the alleyway. She fixed her eyes on Owers, and tripped, almost fell alongside him. She made wheezing sounds as she pushed and pulled at his body.

It was the movement of Miss Post

putting Tad back down, that caught the old woman's attention. Her face was sickly and withered, and she couldn't find words to express herself.

Tolman, who'd replaced his gun, was eyeing the gathering crowd. He was nervous, but at the same time relieved to have the attention diverted. There were a few moments of distressing silence, and then Miss Post turned away. Ushering Tad, she slowly stepped the few paces back to the hotel entrance.

She glanced at Jake as she passed by. He wanted to reach out and give her reassurance, but withdrew from the irony. He cursed bitterly under his breath, looked back to the group of people in the street.

Meg Owers had been helped to her feet, and she turned stiffly to face Tolman. 'I'm not blamin' you, Mr Tolman,' she said sniffling. 'I told him . . . told the old goat that one day that cannon would get him killed.'

Nervous sweat ran down Tolman's

face and he gulped, nodded. 'Take him inside,' he told two men who'd arrived along the sidewalk.

They were HOG 'punchers and, as they indolently picked up the body of Tom Owers, Jake felt the bile rise in his throat. What Meg Owers had to say sickened him, and he felt anger and revulsion for Roach Tolman.

There'd be no court hearing. Jake knew that any worthy law process would be avoided. Tolman carried the protection of Hiram Galt, and in Bullhead, Galt was the law.

A vein pulsed in Jake's temple. He started to consider the Willems' inevitable encounter with the HOG spread.

3

Provocation

Meg Owers had been right. By always carrying the old handgun, her Tom had finally and fatally tempted fate. In small groups, the townsfolk talked out their bad feelings. In the White Glass Saloon, Jake Willem heard whisperings that would have unsettled Tolman. He also noticed that some HOG riders were avoiding town.

So far as he knew, there'd only been four witnesses to the shooting — Rosie Post, Meg Owers and himself, as well as Tad. Jake doubted there'd be any form of hearing, that he'd be called upon to testify. In that town, lawful process was within the gift of Hiram Otto Galt.

He did consider going home. Jess would say it wasn't *his* business, and to walk away. Because of the animosity between him and the HOG foreman, Jake wasn't doing much talking, making new friends. He was a witness and knew the truth of Tom Owers' death. There were many townsfolk who'd worry about the style and scope of Hiram Galt's revenge if Jake Willem did take the stand.

★   ★   ★

Grip Basin was flushed crimson when eight HOG riders rode into Bullhead.

With his head dipped against the setting sun, Jake reached for his makings, made a cigarette to conceal his interest. 'The circus without its clown,' he murmured, as he watched Hiram Galt leading them in.

The man was riding a buckboard, his hands expertly jiggling the reins of a claybank mare. Alongside him rode a boy with equal, sure bearing. Jake recognized him as the son, Tyler Galt.

Jake watched until the riders reached the corral that adjoined the livery stable. Then he crossed the street, to the hotel. On those nights when the HOG outfit was in town, he knew that to wander too freely was a call for trouble — even without Roach Tolman.

The lobby in the Twist Wind was unlit and the dining room was gloomy. A little early maybe, Jake thought, and he pulled a rocker over to one of the front windows. He made another cigarette and, as he smoked, he wondered if Rosie Post was around, how much longer she'd be staying in Bullhead.

It was the sound of a bell that interrupted his thinking. He opened his eyes, looked up to see Tyler Galt closing the front door behind him. From half-a-dozen paces, Jake saw how slight he actually was. With his long curly hair, and standing in the shadows, he didn't look too far off boyhood.

As Tyler peered across the room, Bill Quarry suddenly appeared from his office. 'Hey, young Tyler, it's good to see you,' he greeted him, and went to light some lamps.

Tyler smiled and raised his hand. As the light spread, he looked around and saw Jake, faltered momentarily. 'I'd like one of Pa's rooms,' he said to Quarry.

'They're all occupied, Tyler. There has been a lot o' you in town.' Quarry sounded almost apologetic, probably because Hiram Galt retained some rooms exclusively for HOG use.

But the youngster didn't seem put out. 'Roach is in town for a few days, isn't he? I'll take his room,' he said. 'He can sleep in the livery stable with the boys.'

Quarry hastily considered HOG's chain of authority. 'Yeah, well, he didn't show up *last* night,' he answered thoughtfully.

'Probably rat-assed,' Tyler shrugged. 'I'll bed down under the sidewalk, then. Ask his family to move over.'

Quarry's mouth opened and his eyes rolled. He knew Tyler was ragging him, but he worried about what Tyler's father would have to say.

'Give him *my* room,' Jake interrupted.

Quarry's shoulders slumped. 'Who was it said, force always loses out to kindness?' he asked, with genuine relief.

'Weren't Hiram Galt,' Tyler quipped. He turned to face Jake, met his gaze with open interest. 'You'll be Jake Willem . . . friend of our foreman,' he said, smiling mischievously. 'I'd like to talk to you for a moment . . . in private,' he added.

Jake was intrigued. He nodded, indicated the other side of the room.

'We had a rider come out to see Pa,' Tyler began. 'Feller said you and the girl who came in on the City stage, saw the shootin'. Is that right? Did you?'

Jake didn't answer. He wondered why Tyler hadn't asked Tolman. But the boy's next question gave him part of the answer.

'Was it Roach? Was he drunk?'

Jake understood that Tyler was looking for something.

'No. He was the worse for it, but not

drunk,' Jake said, and continued, 'If he *had* have been, would it have made a difference?' he asked.

'Could be, yeah. Did the girl provoke him?'

Jake knew then what was wanted. It was the start of Galt pressure, and it irritated him. 'Tolman didn't need provocation,' he snapped. 'Old Tom Owers could hardly stand. It was as close to murder as you'll ever get to see. You got yourself a real fur-trimmed hero in Roach Tolman, kid.'

Tyler was visibly taken aback. He clenched his fists and stared uncomfortably at Jake.

'An' as for Miss Post, she was mindin' her own. She had the kid with her, for Chris'sakes,' Jake furthered. 'You Galts can sleep easy though,' he ended scornfully, 'knowin' that my evidence won't be hangin' him. Not here in Bullhead.'

But Tyler Galt didn't seem to be listening. 'I'll not waste any more o' your time, Mr Willem,' he mumbled.

'I'll thank you for the room, an' say goodnight.'

Jake stayed for a couple of house whiskies with Quarry. Both men agreed that Hiram Galt would ply Meg Owers with ample dollars for continued silence. The case would rest as self-defence. As neat an open-and-shut case as was never heard.

Using back alleys, carefully avoiding the main street, Jake made his way to the livery stable. He checked over the mules, and with a blanket from under the driving seat, rolled into a hay pile for the night.

4

The Canner

It was late afternoon the following day, and back at Two Jays, Jake was long overdue. He knew that if he didn't return with the ranch supplies soon, Jess would be coming after him. But he was reluctant to go back directly, so he strolled along to the White Glass Saloon. He played solitaire for an hour, then went to the livery stable. He was working on the harness, buckling a mule collar, when he heard voices from outside.

'Doc's got the rig, ma'am. Wouldn't trust you with anythin' else — not with the kid an' all,' Muggs Chaffey, the stableman was saying. 'What would you be wantin' out at the Catkin, ma'am . . . don't mind me askin'?'

'I'd be *wanting* it, because I *own* it,'

24

Rosie Post said simply.

'Yes, ma'am, you own it,' Chaffey confirmed, not entirely hiding his surprise.

Jeez, that's it, Jake thought, and immediately wondered why it hadn't occurred to him before. The lady owned property, *and* within five miles of Two Jays. A fork of Oglala Creek, and a swathe of birch would be all that divided them. It's a good start, he was thinking, when Roach Tolman spoke up.

'You got possession o' Silas Bench's place? You must've got a good price. Buy it unsighted, did you?'

'I'm not sure I want to answer any of those questions, Mr Tolman,' Rosie Post replied tartly. 'No doubt you have a reason for asking them?'

That's it, Tolman, Jake sniggered in silence, devastate her with your charm. He grinned and walked quietly to be nearer the stable door.

'I'm just interested, ma'am,' Tolman said, without sounding too perturbed. 'I

know Mr Galt had a run in with Bench
. . . wanted him out o' the basin, 'cause
of it.'

'That's of no interest to me,' Rosie
continued tersely.

Jake edged closer to the doorway as
Tolman went on.

'Come visit the HOG, ma'am, why
don't you? There might be somethin' of
interest out *there*. You can take your
pick o' the best beef.'

Jake swore silently at Tolman's
boorishness. But Rosie was still in
control.

'If you mean what I think you mean,
Mr Tolman, let me tell you I've seen
better meat spooned from a tin can,'
she jibed.

Jake chuckled and stepped outside.
Chaffey had backed off, was securing
the gate of the freighter. To Jake's
surprise, the boy Tad was on board,
thrashing air with a willow switch.

'Miss Post's sure got a way with
words, Tolman,' he said, with a sneaky
smile. Then he turned to Rosie Post. 'I

can take you and the boy out to the Catkin,' he said. 'You can see I got space, an' it's more or less the way I'm headed.'

At that, Tolman railed. 'Right now, there's only one way you're headed, mister,' he rasped. 'An' I'm goin' to have to show you where.'

There was upset then, in Rosie's voice. 'I don't want to be the cause of any more trouble in this town. I — '

Jake had already taken off his coat, was unbuckling his gunbelt. 'You won't be,' he cut in. 'This time it's served up by Tolman here. What say you get some dirt off the mud, puppy? Perhaps Muggs can work the pump for you.'

Rosie understood the situation, and so helped Tad from the wagon. Tolman was glaring at Jake, as the inevitability of his threat sank in.

Jake indicated the livery stable. 'In here,' he snapped impatiently.

The purpose was clear, and removing his own jacket and Colt, the HOG foreman followed inside.

Jake pulled off his hat, rolled his gun into his coat and dropped the bundle on the ground. He led his mules outside, told Chaffey to harness them up. 'If the legs hold out, shouldn't be more'n a couple o' minutes,' he said.

In the stable, Tolman looked around, hung his gun on a nail. 'For me this'll be for the lady's hand. What's in it for you, old man?' he asked, as Jake returned.

Jake shook his head. 'To change the shape o' your face, you son-of-a-bitch.'

As always, when Tolman's temper broke, his impulse was to hurt. The man took a noisy intake of breath and rushed forward.

Jake crouched and took Tolman just above the knees, raised his back as he felt contact. Losing his footing, Tolman went up and over Jake's back. He tried to break his fall but failed, landed heavily on his shoulder and face in the hard muck.

Jake was standing with his hands at his sides when Tolman came to his feet.

The man gave a grunt and heaved his shoulders. Then he ducked his head and wiped a hand across his nose and forehead, saw the smear of blood on his shirt sleeve.

'You're leakin' gravy, meat head,' Jake snorted. 'Come try again.'

The low sound of anger rose in Tolman's throat as he came in. His first step was almost cautious, but then more reckless. Jake punched him hard in the face, elbowed him in the ribs, as he stepped nimbly aside. Then he caught Tolman behind the ear with the edge of his hand as the man lunged past.

Tolman wheeled and charged in again. His arms were flailing now though, and his breath came in laboured sighs.

Jake was beat for speed and agility. But their reaches were about the same, and he carried the weight advantage, knew how to use it. He also knew that if he marked up Tolman's face too much, he'd suffer a deadly payback sometime.

So, with his left hand, he piled a big fist into Tolman's belly. When the man's chin hit the point of his shoulder, he matched the punch with his right.

He broke away, ducked Tolman's unsound attempt at a bear hug. But Tolman, thinking his man was evading him, went for another attack.

But Jake had had enough. He saw the opening and drove in a hefty right. With all his weight he caught Tolman on the side of his head. The man twisted sideways, and Jake kicked him, helped him to the ground.

With an ugly sobbing noise, Tolman lay on his side, gagging for air. Jake moved towards him, and noticed Rosie Post standing to one side of the doorway.

'Get the kid back up on the wagon,' he said, reluctantly harsh.

A startled look came into Rosie's eyes, but she quickly stepped away when Jake looked back to Tolman.

'Get to your feet!' Jake said sharply.

The man rolled over onto his knees,

and with his back to Jake, rose unsteadily. Trying to keep his feet outspread, he wheeled awkwardly. Sick disappointment filled his eyes, and his chest was heaving with the effort of taking in air.

For a few, still seconds, the two men watched each other.

'I'm goin' home, Tolman,' Jake said, calmly. 'You could be headed for one o' them Chicago cannin' factories. Make up your mind.'

With a slow festering gesture, Tolman rubbed at his jawbone. Then he took his coat, and walked from the barn into the approaching dusk.

Wearily Jake shrugged into his own jacket. 'An' I thought *mules* were meant to be stupid,' he sniffed. 'It sure ain't easy bein' a poor hay shaker.'

Outside, he pushed his head into the water trough, pulled away spluttering and blinking. Rosie Post and the boy were standing in front of him. He eyed Tad. 'It's somethin' that dumb men do . . . a sort of arguin',' he said, with a painful-looking grin.

Rosie smiled tormentedly. 'We'll be obliged for the ride out to Catkin, Mr Willem,' she said, 'me and Tad.'

'The name's Jake.'

'I know. I'm Rosie.'

Jake ran his fingers through his hair. 'Oh, I know that,' he laughed. 'If you've baggage to pick up, I'll be waitin' outside o' the hotel in twenty minutes.'

5

Bushwhack

Heading east, through the basin, Jake Willem's freighter rolled through lush, wheat grass. The Black Hills lay to the north, the highest peaks still white with lingering snow.

'Not all things seem so important . . . so great, when you're in country like this,' Rosie said.

'An' what *things* would they be?' Jake asked.

'Being labelled some sort of scapegrace for the holding of a child's hand.'

'I heard you tell Quarry, Tad was your nephew.'

'He *is*, but who'd believe it?'

Jake listened with concern and some concealed interest. '*I did*. So, what else is there?' he asked.

'Well, the street-fighting . . . men

killing each other. An' I don't think Meg Owers is painting a fair portrait of me. She's got good cause not to.'

'Sorry Rosie, but men been fightin' each other long before you arrived. Last Thanksgivin' dinner at the Twist Wind, a feller was gut shot for stealin' the pope's nose. An' as for ol' Tom's death, I'm sure you can live with the truth o' that.'

After a thoughtful silence, Jake pointed out the Two Jays ranch as the wagon topped a rise. 'Anyways,' he said, 'there ain't *too* many folk without a wrongdoin' to their name. Not here in the basin.'

The Catkin ranch lay ahead of them, and after another fifteen minutes, Jake walked the mules through an over-grown kitchen garden. There was a barn and two sheds. A corral edged a small log house and a run-around stream.

'Did you notice any livestock on the bill o' sale?' Jake asked, as he drew the wagon to a halt.

Rosie laughed. 'There was mention

of some cattle, a few saddle-brokes and a work team, under 'goodwill'.'

'Hmm. Well, we can tally the cows, after we found 'em. They probably gone fence crawlin'. Jess can help you clear up, do some mendin',' Jake offered.

Rosie was lifting Tad down from the wagon. 'Haven't you got your own ranch to run?' she asked.

'I've got a herd o' mixed stock on it's way up from the North Platte. Until it gets here, there ain't much to do. Jess probably took his rod to the creek, the moment I left for Bullhead.'

'There must be one or two things. And for that I'm grateful,' Rosie said. 'But for the time being, we'll get by. I'd prefer it that way.'

'Didn't know there was ranchin' around Pierre? Jake said, surprisedly. 'You don't look like a farmer's kid.' Jake smiled, shook his head as he pulled down a rope-bound chest.

Rosie handed Tad a carpet bag. 'I'm not,' she replied. 'I'm the daughter of a boat builder. Pa made musselers.

Fashioning land can't be that much more difficult.'

Jake lifted a hand. 'I wouldn't know about that, Rosie. But there's some folk around here find mendin' *boots* a challenge.'

Rosie turned to Jake and gave him a serious smile, indicated for Tad to go to the house. 'Let me tell you about me,' she said. 'I know you must have been wondering.'

'Can't deny that, Rosie, but it don't mean I have to know.'

'I'm going to tell you, anyway,' she said. 'At least the bits about why I'm here.' They both leaned against the freighter. Jake made a cigarette, while Rosie told her story.

'One Christmas, some neighbours had family come down from near Gettysburg. Saffy — that's my sister, Saffron — met and fell for one of them. His name was Derram Kale. Pa found out and tried to stop it, but Saffy took to the river. Pa never spoke of her again . . . said Derram was a 'no-good'. He died two years later. That's when I had to go looking for Saffy.

'Derram was master of a mail packet. It plied between Fort Thompson and Bismark . . . through the lakes. There was a bad storm and the boat ran into rocks. He was drowned, north of Whitlocks crossing.'

For a few moments, Rosie stopped talking. She was collecting her emotions before continuing. 'Tad was only a few months old. The Postal League made a collection for Saffy, but it wasn't much. She wasn't going to ask for money, not from anyone. I cared for her when she got ill, even took her to an infirmary near Mitchell. That's where she died.

'I decided to move east . . . bring Tad with me,' she said quietly, after another long moment. 'I wasn't going back to Pierre. There was no one else.'

'I didn't have to be told all that, Rosie,' Jake said. 'But Jess'll be pleased. He was askin'. He don't know too much about — '

' — Fallen women? And you?' Rosie asked.

'I'm pleased you fell into Grip Basin,' he answered, accepting how much he was getting to like the girl from Pierre. 'It's a community improvement all right. An' that herd I was tellin' you about? Well, that's real quality, too,' he enthused. 'An' some o' the men'll want to stay on. Like you, they know good land when they see it.'

★ ★ ★

'Hey, take it easy,' Jake called, as the wagon pulled back up the rise. The team was eager as they headed for home, and his muscles strained as he hauled the lines back.

They were trotting down the east, home side of the slope when, from the edge of the timber, the crack of a rifle shot split the evening air.

As the noise reverberated around him, Jake felt the thump in his left side. The hot black wave hit him, for a moment knocked him away from full consciousness. 'Christ, you're a bad loser, Tolman,' he groaned.

He rolled into the back of the freighter as another shot rang out. 'I'm already hit, you bastard,' he shouted angrily, as the bullet splintered a side board. He turned onto his side, saw blood welling above his gunbelt. 'Run, Dutch,' he shouted, switched the lines to his right hand as a third bullet ripped into a grain sack, beside his face.

On the near side, Dutch squealed. Jake guessed by the sudden swerve of the wagon that his lead mule had been hit. But then the team broke into a gallop down the slope, and Jake was thrown against the side of the freighter. The pain from his side was agonizing when the next bullet tore into the wagon. It smashed his foot and he loosened his hold on the lines. 'Yeah, you got me,' he hissed, as his head dropped into the spilled grain.

Within minutes, the stricken freighter was onto flat grassland, the mules in a long nervy run for Two Jays.

6

Opening Shoot

At the Willems' cabin, the mules swerved widly across the hard-pummelled yard. The drumming hoofs, the snap and tear of strained traces had brought Jess running. He grabbed at the bridle of Dutch, clung on, as the wounded mule plunged and reared. He dug his heels into the ground, for a long minute, breathed heavy while Dutch puffed anxiously.

Holding the bridle in his left hand Jess stepped back a pace, saw the dark blood and sweat, the wound in the muscles of Dutch's chest. He grabbed out at the panel of the wagon with his free hand, drew himself in close enough to look over.

At the sight of his father lying face-down among the sacks and boxed supplies, Jess cursed and dropped the lines. 'I'm lettin' go. Cause a fuss, an' it really will be crow-bait,' he yelled at the mules.

He turned Jake over, gently moved his arm away from his side. From beneath Jake's body, blood had run into the cracked boards of the wagon floor. He pushed his fingertips up under his pa's chin, deep into his throat. 'Saw you do somethin' like this to a bum calf once,' he muttered, as he felt for a pulse.

Jess saw the bullet that had ripped through Jake's right foot. He gulped at the bloodied mess of bone and leather, and yelled for Edson. Among the ranch help's grips was a leather valise, and he sometimes talked of flesh and blood workings. It was knowledge enough for Jess.

'Pa's been shot up bad. We got to get him inside,' Jess shouted, as he pulled out the tailgate. 'Looks like someone was tryin' to break up our wagon, too.'

As Jess reached for his pa's shoulders, he glanced along the high ground. Far along the wagon road and across the treeline, a disturbed hawk had spiralled upwards from a pine-topped butte.

As Jess and Edson carried Jake to the cabin, Jake groaned and his eyes opened. 'Can't feel my goddamn foot,' he grated.

'That's 'cause most of it's back in the wagon. 'We're gettin' you inside, so Ed can sew up what's left.'

As soon as they'd laid Jake on his bed, Edson went to the barn for his bag. 'I ain't got much. Don't look like we'll be needin' any bone saws,' he said.

An hour later, and Jess had finished cleaning the wound below Jake's ribs. His pa twisted his head, the spear of pain bringing back sharpness.

'What's happened, Jess? I'm tellin' you, I can't feel a thing.'

'There's a bullet wound in your side, but it ain't much. Ed's done some neat work on your foot, but you ain't goin'

to be kickin' up your heels for a spell.'
He smiled affectionately. 'Is that what
you been doin' in town, Pa?'

'In one way. I reckon I got me some
sort o' lady trouble,' Jake grimaced.
'Her name's Rosie Post . . . new owner
o' Silas Bench's place. That's where I've
been . . . with her an' the kid . . . takin'
'em to their new home.'

Jess's face moved with bewilderment.
'That really don't make too much
sense, Pa. Let's just talk some more,
until Ed's firewater gets to you.'

Lacking detail, Jake gave a faltering
but intriguing account of his exploits in
Bullhead. But eventually, Edson's warm
whiskey brew got a firmer grip on him.
'I'm real tired, Jess. What you thinkin'?'
he sighed.

'I'll tell you, Pa. Then we talk it over
later,' Jess said quietly, understanding
his father's weariness. 'Hiram Galt ain't
out to make anyone's life any easier. If
Two Jays an' Catkin get cosied up, he
might worry about some o' the other
ranchers doin' likewise.'

Jess watched his father's face closely as he carried on. 'I don't see what Galt can do to us. He's got the size all right, but we own Two Jays like he owns HOG. You reckon it was Roach Tolman who fired on you?'

'No, not really. He wouldn't've been up to sittin' on the can, let alone a saddle.' Jake closed his eyes again and Jess leaned in close.

'I'm ridin' over to Catkin. I'd like to meet this new lady friend o' yours,' he said. 'Pretty soon, your foot's goin' to give you some real bad moments. Ed's gettin' somethin' to make it easier.' Now he saw that Jake was close to sleep.

Jess lifted the lid of a cabin trunk, quietly removed the double-barrelled fowler and a box of cartridges. He took a long, hard look at his father then at Edson, who'd returned from tending the mules.

Edson nodded back his understanding of what Jess intended to do. 'You go careful, young Jess. I ain't got enough physic for the two o' you,' he said.

As Jess closed the door behind him, Edson started to refill the night lamps. He, too, wondered who'd laid the bushwhack for Jake Willem.

7

Hog-Tied

Muggs Chaffey splashed water on Roach Tolman's face until he got a response. 'Musn't laugh ... ain't funny,' he said, recalling the fate of old Tom Owers.

Tolman's belly hurt, his face was throbbing and his right eye was swollen. He groaned and supported himself uneasily on an elbow. 'Did she go with him?' he demanded of the stableman.

Chaffey nodded hesitantly, and Tolman swore. 'Get me some drinkin' water,' he snarled.

For some time, Tolman dabbed at his face, but couldn't conceal the swelling. Eventually he pushed his Colt back into his holster and picked up his hat. 'Tell Fole Stiller, I want to see him right away. He'll be in the White Glass,' he rasped at Chaffey.

* * *

'Some other time you'd've skinned him.' Stiller lightly mocked Roach's account of the beating he'd taken. 'An' if Willem ain't in town . . . ?'

'He'll be somewhere between here an' the ranch. Just find him,' Tolman hissed. 'Then ride on, an' get me the stallion. Bring it back to HOG.'

Stiller flicked dirty straw from the toe of his boot. 'What about his boy? He's likely to be around . . . proddy too.'

Tolman swore. 'If he tries to stop you, bury him.'

'My tough luck, an' your tough talkin'. All this for a woman an' a horse. You sure it's worth it, Roach?'

Stiller saw the answer in Tolman's bitter, humourless eyes. 'I'd best get goin' then,' he said.

Tolman followed Chaffey's tracks to the White Glass Saloon. As he put his hand up to the batwing doors, he turned to see a HOG cowboy hurrying towards him.

'Been lookin' for you, boss,' the man said, thoughtfully eyeing his foreman. 'The old man wants to see you. He's at the agency.'

At HOG's cattle office, Tyler Galt was looking from a window out onto the street. He turned, but said nothing when Tolman entered. At his desk, Galt senior was equally silent, his weathered features unmoving.

Tolman met the rancher's calculating eyes, looked down at Tom Owers' cherished old pistol. 'Is this supposed to mean somethin'?' he grated uneasily.

Galt's dark eyes moved again, swung up to study Tolman's bruised features. 'Meet up with a friend o' the Owers' family?' he asked acidly.

'Just say what you got to say,' Tolman said.

'If it had been anyone other than one o' my men who'd pulled that stunt with Owers, they'd be stretchin' hemp,' Galt snapped back. 'You're good enough with that piece o' yours to have hit him in the arm or leg. You'd certainly have had time.'

Tolman's face coloured. He started off with a defence, realized he didn't have one. 'Chaffey came straight to you, didn't he? I'll remember that,' he said.

'Muggs is answerable to me!' Galt commanded. 'You'll put that Post woman out of your mind, too. You're paid to keep trouble away, Roach, not to bring it on home. I ain't happy.'

'I wouldn't've said Rosie Post was much trouble, Pa,' Tyler offered. 'She's kind o' pretty too.'

Galt looked enquiringly at his son. 'What do you know of her?' he asked.

'We've met.'

'When?'

'This mornin' at the hotel. She said she had some stuff for the mail coach. There was no one to look after the kid. I was in the hall and said I'd help.'

'What the hell do you know about tendin' chits?' Galt was surprised.

'Not much. She never took me up on it.'

'I'm not surprised. You're only just out o' breeches yourself. What did you do then?' Galt asked, curiously interested.

Tyler flashed a short, cheeky look at his father. 'I just hung around.'

Galt went quiet for a second, then nodded perceptively. 'Yeah, well, you steer clear o' this girl until we know more about her.'

Tolman grunted. '*What* more? Where's the snotnose's ma an' pa? Why'd she buy Catkin without seein' it? Where'd she get the money? What's goin' on?'

Galt's voice revealed his irritation. 'Has anyone ever questioned you on your folks, Roach?' he asked slow and meaningfully.

'She's only just got into town,' Tyler said. 'What's she supposed to do? Take out a notice in the *Bullhead Banner*?

Not that it would have helped *you* much,' he added.

Galt relaxed, even grinned a little. He looked at his foreman and shrugged, placed his hands flat on his desk. Then he picked up Owers' old pistol and dragged at the rusty mechanism. 'I want you to stay another night in town, Roach. Tomorrow, you're goin' up to check on the summer graze. You can send Leggs back.'

Tolman's expression turned hostile. 'Why?' he demanded.

'Because I said so. There's one or two things need doin' without your kind o' help. Now make up your mind, Roach,' Galt challenged. 'It's out on HOG pasture or inside a county jail. Make your choice.'

Tolman knew he couldn't push Galt too far, that there'd be no compromise. It was time for him to give way and both men knew it. He considered his longer term prospects, his life without the customary HOG benefits. 'I guess you're right, boss,' he said, as he turned to the door.

'Of course I am, Roach. You just gave up on knowin' it for a while,' Galt told him.

8

Out of Salts

Jess Willem was normally possessed of an open, cheery nature, but when he thought about the hidden rifleman, his temperament became less obliging. It crossed his mind that whoever had fired at his pa, might still be hidden in the trees, and there *he* was, presenting an inviting figure against the skyline.

But he got more relaxed as he rode creekside through the timberline. Behind and below him, the fast-running water rippled a shiny ribbon. That was when his horse decided to lower its head into the Oglala, snort wildly at the sudden chill. Jess reined in as the horse lost its footing. It took fright and plunged forward, then twisted, turned back and ran.

As Jess fell from the saddle, he

groped wildly at the tangle of roots between rocks and moss-covered crevices. He smacked into the creek and went under, fought his way back to the surface. The water was enervating and he'd hit his head. Struggling against the spike of pain, he clawed towards the trees along the bank. He straightened up when he felt bottom, groped his fingers around the low overhang of a gnarled pine. He pulled himself up and onto the rocky bank, for a moment lay sodden and bone-chilled.

Against the noise of his teeth rattling he thought he heard a noise. He waited and, not forgetting the shotgun, wondered where his horse had got to. He clambered to his feet, brushed at the watery blood that ran from his forehead.

'What happened?' the boy said. He was standing twenty feet away, holding the reins of his own mount and Jess's mare. 'I'm Tyler Galt.'

'I got thrown . . . my fault,' Jess

answered directly. 'What's a Galt doin' up here?'

'Takin' the short route between Bullhead and HOG,' Tyler Galt said. 'Who are *you*?' he asked, sounding like he'd guessed the answer. 'How come we never met?'

'I'm one o' the Two Jays . . . Jess Willem, an' I ain't made town too often. Galts an' Willems ain't known for their neighbourliness.' Jess looked interestedly at the mount Tyler Galt had been riding. 'The wagon road's a darn sight easier on a horse,' he remarked.

' 'Tis if you ain't got one that's thrown a shoe.'

Jess stepped forward and picked up his hat. 'Maybe you should've gone back,' he said. 'It's still more'n five miles on to your place. You seen . . . heard anyone else up here?'

'Nothin' except you. Expectin' someone?'

'No, not really. Don't matter none,' Jess said, believing the boy. '*I* can make it on foot to where I'm goin', you can't.

55

Take *my* horse.'

Tyler Galt gave a slight, quizzical smile. 'That don't seem right. Not on what I been told,' he said.

'Ha. Forget what you been told an' take the horse. You met my pa in town?'

'I did, yeah, like most folk. Heard about his bay, too.'

'Just so you don't make him an offer.' Jess walked to his horse, pulled the fowling piece from its scabbard. 'What about your own mare?' he asked.

'She'll follow on . . . won't be any trouble. Where'll you be?' Tyler wanted to know.

Jess studied the wet cling of his garb doubtfully. 'I *was* on the way to Catkin. I'm thinkin' there's trouble headed that way.'

★ ★ ★

Two Jays' yard looked deserted when Fole Stiller approached. He rode around to the rear of the cabin and dismounted, looped the reins of his horse at the small corral. He looked at the bay, then walked to the nearest window, looked into the cookery.

He turned along the side of the cabin, carefully eased back a slatted shutter. On a table he could see a bag and some small bottles. Jake Willem lay on a cot that had been pushed into a corner. The man's eyes were closed, and he was bootless. He'd been bandaged around his middle and his right foot was wrapped tightly in bloodied cotton strips. He appeared to be well asleep.

Stiller turned and stared into the distance, allowed himself a sly grin. He'd seen Jake Willem's boy riding towards the Catkin ranch. So now he'd have the time he needed.

He quickly went back to the corral where Jake Willem's stallion was snatching at pin grass with a few other horses. The bay lifted his head suspiciously as Stiller got close, but the HOG man was good with livestock. The stallion was generally suspicious of strangers, but offered little defiance at Stiller's approach. It bared its teeth and gave a perfunctory kick, then allowed itself to be separated from the others.

Instinct and the chink of spurs stirred Jake from his pain-induced slumber. 'That you Ed . . . Jess?' he called.

But it was Fole Stiller who was staring down at him. 'Have to fight you off, did she?' he asked offensively.

'You'd know it,' Jake answered, as he recognized Tolman's ranny.

'I ain't certain which way to take that, Willem. But if you been gun-fightin', it ain't nothin' to do with me,' he lied. 'I'm here on Roach Tolman's business,' he added, more truthfully.

'I've took care of my dealin's with *him*. What you doin' in my house?' Jake demanded.

'I just said. Tolman sent me for the bay.' Stiller pulled a roll of notes from a pocket, tossed them onto Jake's cot. 'There's two hundred an' fifty dollars,' he said.

On the far side of the cot, Jake was

stretching his hand down to the floor. 'I wonder if the Tolman species ever will survive,' he groaned. Then he looked sternly at Stiller. 'Take the goddamn money back to him.'

If only Stiller had known of the loss of Tolman's status with Galt, he might have done just that. It was normal for him to ride the trail between Tolman and Galt, to satisfy one without crossing the other. But it was plain on his face that a close-up killing was different from the work of a rifleman. 'I was sent to fetch the bay,' he insisted.

As for Jake, he knew that he and Jess were involved in more than a struggle for ownership of a fine stallion. All the same, he wasn't going to let anyone take his horse, and he stretched out his fingers as he moved.

A creak of the cot frame warned Stiller. Jake had rolled from the cot, got to half standing. He backed against the log wall for support, found he couldn't raise his heavy Colt.

Stiller's own gun came up and,

unable to react, Jake felt it pound into his jaw. With one hand clutched painful and useless across his chest, he went heavily down to the floor. He landed on his wounded side, drew in his knees, and made a useless sideways move to rise again. Stiller lashed out with his boot that caught him hard in the shoulder, pointed the barrel of his Colt between Jake's eyes.

But Jake knew that Stiller was a long way from pulling the trigger. If the man was a cold-blooded killer, he'd be dead already. 'I'll see you in hell, mister,' he said, as he fell into his agonized blackness.

Neither man had heard the riders' approach, or saw the three people who were standing in the cookery doorway. Rosie Post had her arms around Tad, Jess Willem was levelling the fowler.

Rosie looked from Jake to Stiller who'd backed himself against the wall. Then she turned to her nephew. 'And now you've met most of our neighbours, Tad,' she said.

Jess puffed air, indicated that Rosie take the youngster outside. Then he stepped in close to Stiller and swung the butt of the fowler low into the man's stomach. As Stiller crumpled, he slammed the barrel across his jaw. 'Shouldn't've shot my pa,' he snarled, and called back Rosie.

Rosie stepped over to Jake. 'Just as well we came back over the ridge,' she said.

Jess carried Jake back to his cot, watched Rosie peel away a wad of dressing. He saw the spread of blood again, gritted his teeth at his father's pastiness and beaded sweat.

'What's goin' to happen to my foot? Tell me the truth, boy . . . you seen how it looks,' Jake said, quiet and breathily.

Jess attempted a hopeful smile. 'You remember that tough old pirate you used to read me about — Long John Silver? Well he was missin' half a *leg*.'

Jake squeezed his eyes shut against the pain. 'An' ended his days with a white-haired lunatic an' a goddamn parrot for company,' he murmured.

As Rosie tugged at an undersheet, Jess noticed the roll of banknotes. He thought for a second, then looked over at Stiller. His face coloured. 'No need to ask our friend here what all this is about,' he said angrily.

Jess stuffed the dollars into Stiller's pocket. Without saying anything more, he dragged the man into the yard, let him lay in the dust while he went to get his horse.

'That's what men do,' Tad called out, as he watched from alongside the front doorway.

For a couple of minutes, Jess busied himself with the roping of Stiller across the back of his horse. Then, giving the boy a long questioning look, he went back inside the cabin.

Rosie was looking at Edson's bottles of salts and iodine spirits. 'There's nothing of much use here. Your pa needs a doctor, Jess. A proper doctor,' she said.

Jess looked hard at the girl. 'I don't

know what's happened to Edson. Can you ride to Bullhead?' he asked. 'It's a lot to ask, specially at full dark. You bein' . . . you know.'

'Yes, I know . . . a lady. I'll be taking *this*, as my beau, then.' Rosie held up Jake's big Colt. 'And it'll come in handy if you let anything happen to young Tad,' she said without jest.

'He'll be all right here. Ain't anyone goin' to pull off a button. But just supposin' the doc refuses to come?'

Rosie's eyes flashed. 'Oh, he'll come, Jess. That's a promise to all of us. Meantime your pa can tough it out.'

Jess smiled his confidence. 'Take the bay,' he said. 'You'll be able to outrun any trouble, if there is any.'

9

The Following Page

Its ears pricked forward, the stallion trotted down the near deserted main street of Bullhead. Rosie took a few deep breaths and walked the horse steady until they closed on the clamour of raised voices, the bawdy laughter that emanated from the White Glass Saloon. She got in close before dismounting at some low steps, then she crossed the boardwalk, and without stopping pushed open the batwing doors. Lit by oil lamps that hung from low rafters, the interior was daunting. The bartender was pressing a sopping rag to the counter top, and he paused to stare open-mouthed at Rosie.

Rosie took a pace inside. With a sniff of offence she smiled. 'Can you tell me where I can find the doctor?' she asked through the mill, and took a step closer.

'Barton Page? Yeah, he's over there.' The bartender wiped his fingers in the dirty cloth as Rosie looked around. 'That's him with the checkered neck-cloth.'

Rosie nodded, gave her thanks and gritted her teeth. For a moment her nerve almost cracked, for it looked like every other man in Grip Basin had chosen that night to visit the bar. She saw a ring of men, two, three deep. One or two were stretching to see over the shoulders of those in front, as she stepped forward.

She avoided eye contact as the men noticed her. Perhaps she could reach Dr Page, make her intentions known before having to ward off a rooster brain.

'Is Dr Page one of you men?' she had to ask the group of card players. 'It's important that I speak to him.'

Two men stood back, and a gap opened between Rosie and the table.

There were four men seated, and one of them was wearing a big silk neckcloth.

'See me in my surgery tomorrow,' the man said. His tone was one of objection and incredulity.

Rosie took a step closer. 'I don't have the time,' she said. 'If *you're* Doc Page, there's a man out at Two Jays who's been shot. He's hurt bad and needs you,' she said hurriedly.

The doctor blew hard. 'Two Jays,' he repeated, his eyes boring into Rosie. 'Willems' place.'

'That makes a difference, does it?' Rosie countered. She hadn't faced up to the consumers of the White Glass for pointless exchanges.

The physician responded stiffly. 'When a callout's involved, it helps for a doctor to know these things.'

Rosie's pulse increased as she realized Page was going to prove difficult. 'We should be leaving,' she said, the worry obvious.

Page snapped his cards face-down on

the table. 'We?' he reiterated. 'I haven't said I'd go anywhere, yet.'

'If you don't come with me, I'll write to every newspaper office between here and Washington. You won't be able to broom a boardwalk in the Dakotas . . . let alone practise medicine.'

Rosie's determined threat seemed to affect everyone in the saloon. 'She threatenin' the doc?' she heard above the coughs, muffled guffaws and low whistles.

Furtively, Page glanced up at the faces looking on.

'Perhaps you'd best take a ride, Bart. She looks madder'n a hornet,' one of his game partners spoke up.

Rosie nodded. 'Madder'n a hornet who carries a great big Colt .44.' She leaned forward, making space. Then she moved her hand down to the deep side-pocket of her riding breeches, saw a change of emotion cross the doctor's face. 'Follow me, Doc. My goodwill just run out.'

The arrogant set of the doctor

disappeared. He picked up his cards and tucked them away inside his jacket. Slowly, he got to his feet. 'Hell, why not,' he relented. 'It's safer than gettin' stung.'

10

The Hog Hollow

Hiram Galt had issued explicit instructions that no one was to accept aid or favour from the Willems. Because of it, Tyler Galt thought it best not to ride Jess Willem's mare all the way home.

When he got to within half a mile of the ranch house, he dismounted in a cottonwood stand. He unsaddled the mare and made a long tether, then, carrying the bridle he set out to walk the rest of the way.

It would be long after dark by the time he got to the yard and most hands would be inside taking supper. He could take a horse from the corral and ride back through the trees to intercept his own horse. Early tomorrow when the coast was clear, he'd take the mare back.

Within an hour he was safely back inside the ranch house. He was studying the cover of a dime novel, when an excited cowboy ran into the kitchen.

'Hey Tyler,' he called out. 'You want to come an' see Stiller. He's been beat . . . got done up like a ring calf.'

'Where is he?' Tyler asked eagerly.

'In the bunkhouse.'

Any more was lost on Tyler. He was already gone, halfway across the yard. He ran at the building, pushed at the half-closed door.

Inside, two HOG men were leaning over a bunk. One of them was holding a lamp.

'What happened, Husky?' Tyler asked him.

'Looks like he been arguin' with the wrong end of a bronc,' the old cowboy replied, dourly.

Stiller looked bad to Tyler. Some of the blood had been washed off, some of it was a filthy smear. His mouth was smashed open, and his nose was

70

messed about, beaten flat against his face.

'Has he said anythin'? Tyler asked.

Husky shook his head. 'Made a few noises.' Before he could say anything more, Stiller opened an eye. It stared angry and bloodshot, and settled on Tyler.

'Get Roach,' he hissed.

Tyler stuttered. 'Wasn't . . . wasn't he with you?'

The beaten man's mouth hardly moved. 'No . . . stayed in town with your pa,' he said thickly and quietly.

Husky said he didn't think a doctor could do much more than dole out a dose of pain-killer. There was no other opinion, so Tyler said the two men ought to do their best until his father returned.

★   ★   ★

After a restive night, Tyler got up early. It was just after first light when his father and Roach Tolman rode in, and his mind was still racing.

But he didn't go out to greet them. He thought there was too much could be said, or *not* said, and he didn't want to lie. He drew his knees up, decided to remain doggo in the armchair.

Tolman and Hiram Galt went straight into Hog Hollow. It was Galt's private lair, led off the south wall of the house. For some time, Tyler listened to the strained conversation between the two men, until grunts and groans meant that Fole Stiller had arrived.

Cussing, he sidled up to the adjoining wall, overcame the embarrassment of snooping when he heard his father's words.

'If Jake Willem kicks off, Stiller, I'll get you dragged to Deadwood. I never knew we'd got to crawl from under rocks to shoot our neighbours down. Because that's what you must've done.'

Tyler could feel his blood racing, tried to remember what Jess Willem had said about trouble. There was another short silence, then Galt carried on.

'Then there was the girl in the saloon. I weren't even into my boots when I learned of it. I heard she put a real interestin' proposition to Doc Page. With you not bein' in town, I sort o' put two an' two together.'

Tyler sniffed quietly. Now he understood what Jess Willem had meant when he'd asked if Tyler had seen or heard anything.

'Willem ain't shot up that bad,' Tolman then joined in. 'It was scarin' stuff. Just enough to make him let that stallion go. Fole didn't — '

'Christ, I should've known *you* figured in it,' Galt snapped back. 'I'd like to have seen that Post girl. Sounds like she's got more sand than you two weasels put together.'

'That *was* the fact of it, Mr Galt,' Stiller insisted. 'I only aimed to crease him. I went to the cabin with Roach's money. Willem hefted a gun when I offered for the horse. I wasn't goin' to get rough.'

'You're carryin' a face like a windfall,

an' *you* weren't goin' to get rough?' Galt roared.

'It was the other one, done that,' Stiller retorted, but more hesitantly. 'He'd rode off to fetch the girl from Catkin. They sneaked back in, an' he caught me cold. Used both ends of a shotgun.'

Galt stared hard at Stiller, shook his head in all sorts of disappointment. 'Most o' that's a goddamn lie. I guess I'll never know the full truth of it,' he said.

'Looks like we've all taken a beatin' for very little,' Tolman said.

'Yeah. You're not only a liability, but a big regret to me, Roach. For young Tyler, too. If only I could be sure you weren't behind it 'cause o' that fat eye Willem gave *you*.'

Tyler tensed at the mention of his name, got ready to move off.

'You *can* be sure, boss,' Tolman came back with. 'I'll get even, face to face. An' Fole would've put killin' lead into Willem if I'd said for him to,' the man went on with his falsehood.

Then the drama got the better of Tyler. He'd had enough, and the fear of being discovered, of listening in on his own father had him away and up the stairs to his own rooms. From what Tolman and Stiller had said, Jake Willem would be laid up for a while.

For half an hour Tyler's mind gave over to rash speculation. Like Jake Willem before him, he ran hot at the thought of a confrontation between the Two Jays and HOG spreads. Then he realized that by taking back Jess's mare, he'd get the chance to talk to Willem.

He heard noises from the yard below and went to his window, saw his father riding from the yard with Roach Tolman and Fole Stiller.

He watched until all three men were well into the home pasture. He felt anger at Roach Tolman. The HOG foreman had let him down, although he wasn't yet ready to believe the man capable of kicking off a murder.

The old man was sending Tolman

and Stiller out to replace a couple of line men up at the summer graze. Tyler knew it was a punishment all right, and a strong one for a foreman and his top hand. His father would ride with them for a few miles, until he'd more fully laid down the law of Hiram Otto Galt.

11

A Recommendation

Apart from a few days of fever and pain, a week's recovery passed without incident for Jake Willem. He didn't take to being laid-up. As soon as he got to his feet without falling down, Jess would probably try and undercut his durability, make light of his toughness.

After cleaning and rebandaging Jake's wounds, Bart Page left behind a bottle of laudanum, and a warning about excessive use. Edson had eventually returned and made up herb and balsam poultices. He applied them liberally to Jake's broken foot and started painful rehabilitation. Jake knew it wouldn't ever be good again, but was confident of getting some feeling and movement back. He spent hours flexing his toes, kneeding the stiff, knotted flesh. From the skin of a deer she'd shot along Oglala Creek, Rosie Post cut and stitched him a tight-fitting sock.

However, Jake knew that as soon as he got his strength back, Rosie would return to her Catkin ranch. Though he and Jess might beat a trail through the treeline, there was no way of knowing what would happen when she was on her own land.

Rosie was more than capable with a rifle. But Jake didn't like her and Tad being alone, thought they were too vulnerable. There was an alternative to a gun for oppression, and Hiram Galt was wily enough to know it.

He considered laying his poorliness on thick, in an attempt to have her stay, but he knew it wouldn't do much for the tainted reputation she already maintained in Bullhead. Not that Jake fretted over such matters, but there were, and would be others, like young Tad Raster to consider.

* * *

Jake's pondering was put aside when, late one day, Jess returned from town excited.

'Galt's sent Tolman and his top hand up to the summer pasture. They must've gone an' done somethin' old man Galt didn't take to,' Jess shouted from astride his chestnut mare.

'When? How'd you know?' Jake asked, limping onto the stoop.

'Bill Quarry told me. I reckon it was just after you got shot up.'

'Yeah, well, the two might be connected,' Jake agreed. 'But I'm also thinkin' o' the Tom Owers' shootin'. I'm thinkin' that if the sheriff o' Rapid City sniffs anythin' on the wind, he might decide to ride over an' ask a few questions hereabouts. If I was Hiram Galt, I'd want to keep things tied down. An' that means Roach Tolman.'

As his son dismounted, Jake saw Rosie walking through the meadow with Tad. 'It would be the end of Galt's judge an' jury days,' he said.

Jess followed his father's gaze, saw

Rosie swinging the kid over the snake fencing into the yard. 'Yeah. He'd've known we weren't up to much. You with your busted foot an' all,' he said. 'He might have considered gettin' rid o' both of us.'

'I don't know about that. There's also Rosie to think about. An' I wager he *does*. An' don't forget the button. How'd he explain that sort o' trouble away?' Jake raised his right hand, greeted Rosie and Tad. 'But our turns'll come, Son. That's as sure as the taxes.'

As Rosie approached, Jess spoke quickly. 'That'll make it difficult for 'em. Bill Quarry also told me, Tolman's sweet on Rosie.'

'Well, ain't we all?' Jake said, with a wry smile. 'That's the trouble with Tolman. He might wear the hat, but it's Galt that's got the cattle.'

Jake was correct in his estimation of Galt's pressure. Within two days of returning home, Rosie Post got herself a visitor at Catkin.

★ ★ ★

It was a fine day, and with Tad beside
her, Rosie ran the buckboard out to
where her home pasture met a bend in
the Oglala. She carried an axe, rope,
and a big Russell knife — all she
needed for making a play raft for Tad.
Jake had advised her not to go
anywhere unarmed, so she tied the
scabbard of her rifle across the rear of
the seat.

In the north-western crook of Catkin
land, Rosie discovered the timber brake
she was looking for. She swung the
long-handled axe, setting to the work
with enthusiasm. 'If I can get the knots
good and strong, Tad, we'll be rafting to
the lakes. Can't figure out a way of
getting back though,' she called out
merrily.

She'd notched birch saplings, was
tugging at rope bindings, when she saw
the rig approaching from the south. The
wagon road that ran through the basin
wasn't visible from where Rosie was

working. It was the route from HOG, on to Two Jays, then Catkin. So whoever it was, had turned off to do more than pass the time of day.

She went and untied the Winchester from the buckboard, took it back to where she was working. She propped it against a stump, told Tad to stay close to the wagon. She was confident enough, but surprised when she saw Hiram Galt himself. As he rode up, she took off a glove, rubbed her wet palm on her hip, pushed back her hat.

'I've come to recommend somethin',' Galt said abruptly, looking for the toughness he'd heard about.

Galt was big, and darkly dressed. Rosie met his piercing eyes without a tremor. 'How did you know I was up here?' she asked.

'In this basin, I know where *most* people are at any given time. I have to keep tabs on my own *kin* sometimes,' Galt replied. He saw the flicker of annoyance in Rosie's eyes. 'An' those who work for me, of course,' he added.

'Of course,' she agreed. 'What's the recommendation you've brought over?'

Galt looked at Tad who was lying on his back, squinting one-eyed at the sky's single cloud. 'I want you to stay clear o' my foreman *an*' Tyler,' he said.

Rosie shook her head, laughed quietly. 'From what little I know of him, Tyler's a nice boy. And will be, for another two or three years.' She stared hard at the ground, thinking of what to say next. 'Roach Tolman? Well he's something else, and I'll not thank you for the thought, Mr Galt.'

'Yeah, Roach is a bone-head, that's for sure. But there's more to be found, deep down,' Galt replied.

'Yes, that's the worrying thing,' Rosie said. 'I'd say you've had a wasted ride.'

Galt wound the reins around the massive span of his hand. 'I'll give you seventeen fifty for this place. That's more than I offered Silas Bench,' he said sharply.

'And less than I paid him,' Rosie retorted, and bent to pick up the rifle when she saw a muscle tighten in Galt's jaw.

'What do you want then?' he demanded impatiently.

Rosie took a deep breath, remained calm. 'What I want, is to be left alone,' she said tolerantly.

'Roach has gone rotten since you came to Bullhead. Whatever you done, you got under his skin, an' there's not many can say that.'

'Oh, I bet there's a breed of chigger that's managed it,' Rosie countered.

Galt snorted angrily. 'Take two thousand an' leave the basin.'

Rosie's patience gave way. 'What I know, and have seen of your foreman, sickens me. Furthermore, I'm not moving from here. Not for you or your money. Now get off my land.'

Galt had another quick glance at Tad. 'Not for long,' he said contemptuously. 'Just remember, I give Roach his good life. But I can send him on his way with nothin' more'n a pair o' rag-assed pants. He won't be comin' to you as a well-gifted suitor.'

'There's sanatoriums in the east for people like you, Mr Galt. You ought to reserve a room while you're still able.' Rosie walked to the buckboard, held out her hand and pulled Tad to his feet.

As Galt swung his rig around, she wondered what was going on out at the HOG. She pushed the rifle into its scabbard, and lifted Tad onto the buckboard. As she went to pick up the axe and knife, she wondered what could have happened to *Mrs* Galt, turned for a last look at the rancher.

'I'll see you in the bedlam o' Bullhead,' he warned.

As she met the chill in Galt's eyes, Rosie thought she had the answer to Mrs Galt.

12

Wanted

Up at the HOG summer pasture, Tolman felt aggrieved and hard done by. Not knowing what was going on around Bullhead, just wore away at him. His face was almost healed, the cracked mouth and swollen eye getting back to normal. Only the damage left inside him by Jake Willem was left to hurt, that and the harm meted out to Fole Stiller.

He had no idea on how Hiram Galt might be dealing with Rosie Post. Any other time, he'd be confident of Galt oiling the waters, ensuring there'd be no serious rival for a girl's attention. He got to thinking about the night just outside of Bullhead when he'd tried to buy the bay from Jake Willem. And in turn, there was the Owers business, followed by the fist fight at Chaffey's livery stable. Rosie Post had been a conspicuous presence on both occasions. So, to Tolman's way of seeing things, with him coming out as a second best, there'd be little rivalry if Willem wanted to make a move for the girl's hand.

Night and day the protagonists emerged, whirled around as figments of Tolman's imagination. Rosie Post, Jake Willem, the big stallion. Tolman's head was exhausted, and he decided to make a move, even take on Hiram Galt and his temper.

But Fole Stiller didn't appreciate the decision. He too had recovered, despite a more heartfelt beating from the younger Willem. His face would bear permanent scars and he'd got deep down belly damage.

The two men sat their saddles while the horses nibbled at the lush grass. Tolman told Stiller what he intended to do.

'You crazy?' Stiller complained. 'The

old man'll fillet us. He said, a *month*.
He didn't mean ten or twelve days.'

'I'll sort *him* out,' Tolman snapped
back. '*You* can stay here. Make a quilt.'

★   ★   ★

Nearly two days later both men reined
in their horses. They stood in the
timber that stretched from the pasture
to within a mile of the HOG ranch
house.

'Goddamnit,' Tolman grunted and
nudged his horse on towards the yard.

The men were turning into the
corral, when Tyler came running from
the house. He stopped short when he
saw them, waited for Tolman as he
started towards the house.

'You're back. Pa said that . . . ' Tyler
started to say, then looked worried.

Tolman pretended not to notice.
'Find me some soap, kid,' he answered.
He walked purposefully to the house.
He thought he'd get scrubbed up, make
it to town before his encounter with

Galt. 'Where *is* he?' he asked casually.

'Pa? He rode out early.' Tyler stepped up alongside Tolman.

'That don't tell me where he is,' Tolman growled, his agitation just sounding.

'He took the wheels to Catkin,' Tyler said cautiously. 'Rosie Post went home. She — '

'Rosie Post?' Tolman called him up short. 'Where'd she been?'

Tyler gave him a sideways look. 'Two Jays. She's been tendin' to Jake Willem.' The boy's face crumpled with the presumption of Tolman's response.

Within seconds the foreman was raging. 'I goddamn knew it. Your pa puts me out to goddamn pasture, an' Willem gets his goddamn feet under the goddamn table.' Then he cursed loudly.

Stiller, who'd been following, got the meaning of Tolman's outburst. 'Goddamn sounds like it,' he muttered, and did a quick turn in the direction of the bunkhouse.

It was different for Tyler. He was safe

from any Tolman retaliation. 'Pa says there's somethin' between Rosie Post an' Jake Willem,' he said, conveying his callow, earthy fascination for the liaison. 'He says you can't control them sort o' things.'

'I'll control 'em. That Willem nest-makin', while I been tallyin' blades o' grass.' Tolman broke off to curse again, his only imminent way of dealing with the turmoil.

'Pa says *you* was to blame, Roach. Says you had it comin'. He had to send you up country for your own good.'

'Sometimes your pa sure says too much for *his* own good, kid,' Tolman sneered.

An hour later, although scrubbed up and neatly outfitted, the ugliness of his mood hadn't changed. He kicked cruelly into the flanks of a fresh mount as he headed for town. He was deliberating his next move, swore dreadful fates on those who got in his way.

★ ★ ★

It was late afternoon when Tolman rode into Bullhead and dismounted at the White Glass's hitching rail. He was earlier than usual, couldn't wait to find out the comings and goings of the past ten days.

One of the few hurdy-gurdy girls wasted no time in siding up to him at the bar. 'You'll get pecked by the bird, if you're not careful, Mr Roach,' she breathed close. 'I ain't even had time to work up a thirst.'

'One drink. I want to talk, that's all,' Tolman said quietly and quickly.

Ten minutes later, Tolman stood alone at the bar. He turned his eye to the early poker game, sauntered over to the table. 'Mind if I sit in?' he asked.

'Pull up a chair, Roach. Looked like you had other things on your mind, for a while there. But your money's just as welcome here.' Doc Page looked at the man sitting next to him. 'If that's agreeable with you, Mr Boone?' he asked.

The stranger tipped his hat, gave a friendly nod.

'This is Mr Boone from Wyoming,' Page said. 'Got here on today's stage.' The doctor looked at Boone. 'This is Roach Tolman. Foreman of the HOG ranch.' He introduced the two men.

Boone stood up and held out his hand. 'Foreman of the HOG, eh?' the man sounded pleased. 'That's a stroke o' luck. It's Hiram Galt I've come all the way from Sheridan to see.'

'My father,' he said, noting Tolman's surprised look. 'Him and Mr Galt were partners. Years ago, they worked a claim in the Black Hills. I've got some very important papers for him. If I ain't pressin' my luck, when were you headin' back to the ranch?' he asked.

Tolman was still curious. 'We *could* leave right now,' he suggested with little conviction.

Boone sat down and smiled good-naturedly. 'We all have a weakness, Mr Tolman. Happily, mine's on the table in front o' me,' he drawled. 'So if you don't mind, an' with me havin' come this far, I'll just indulge myself for a while longer.'

The game lasted until daybreak the following morning. Grip Basin was shrouded in its deep carpet of mist, when Tolman and Boone walked stiffly from the saloon. Tolman found a saddle horse at Chaffey's stable, then called them up a breakfast at the hotel. It was still early when the two men rode for the HOG.

Tolman was ill at ease, bothered about the man from Sheridan. For the first time, found the game of poker tiresome. But he'd had time to think, now wanted to be alone with Boone to pose a question or two.

But his anxiety wasn't going to be sated just yet. Tolman reined in, when he was waved down by Fole Stiller. HOG's top hand was on his way to a grub house at the far end of town. He stepped into the street, held the bridle of Tolman's horse.

'I followed you in,' he said, before

Tolman could ask the question. 'I weren't goin' to get bull tailed by the old man, if an' when he turned up. That's for *you* to deal with, Roach.'

Tolman swore silently to himself. He didn't want to upset Stiller. The two men had too much on each other to hold more than a petty grudge.

Boone sensed the mood. 'Some sort o' problem?' he asked.

'Nothin' to concern you,' Tolman said quickly as he pulled his horse away.

★   ★   ★

Tolman made little and awkward conversation on the ride out to HOG. And Boone didn't offer any more of an explanation for his visit.

As soon as they rode into the ranch yard, Tolman shouted, 'Husky, come an' take care of these horses. An' where's the boss?' he asked anxiously.

'He rode out to see Earnley. He's fillin' the line shacks with winter feed stuff.'

Tolman's pulse raced. Grif Earnley and Galt had known each other for many years, were close, old-time friends. Tolman realized then, that something was going on, and that by Galt's rights, it should be going on without him.

He guided Boone towards the house, led him up on to the veranda. He opened the heavy oak door, indicated that Boone should enter.

Tolman pushed the door to behind them. 'Now, Mr Boone from Sheridan,' he said confrontationally. 'You were sayin' your pa an' Hiram Galt were partners?'

Boone nodded. 'That's what I said, yeah. High on the Cheyenne. Is there somethin' wrong?'

'There is, Mr Boone. Somethin' very wrong. You see, Hiram Galt's always been a cattle rancher. He ain't ever pan washed, let alone worked a goddamn claim. In fact, 'an inch o' gold don't buy an inch o' time' is one of his favoured old saws.' Tolman drew his plated Colt, pushed the barrel up close to Boone's nose. 'Now you tell me what you want, Mr Boone, or I'll put another hole in the front o' your face.'

'My name *is* Boone . . . Henry Boone, and I *am* here to see Hiram Galt. The rest was flummery for the good doctor . . . them I was playin' with.'

Tolman sniffed. 'That game's over. Get on with it,' he said.

'Hiram Galt's the man who can help me find who I'm lookin' for. I was told that, by a colleague in Rapid City.' Boone eyed Tolman carefully. 'An' that's all I'm goin' to say.'

Tolman smiled nastily, eased back the hammer of the Colt.

Boone looked suitably troubled. 'Perhaps it'll make more sense if I show you a credential,' he suggested.

Boone took a step back. 'I should've guessed,' he said. You're a lawman.'

'Not quite. I'm a representative of a Missouri River Detective Bureau. You wouldn't've heard of us.'

'No I wouldn't. But maybe I know who you're lookin' for,' Tolman said, his mind suddenly racing. 'So, tell me his name, goddamnit.'

'It's a woman. She's young, dark, could pass for an injun if it weren't for her eyes. She's got a younker in tow.'

'Her name?' Tolman asked, slowly lowering his gun from Boone's face.

'Swann. Martha Rosemary Swann. An' over in Mitchell, she's wanted for murder.'

13

The Whole Truth

Rosie Post ran the buckboard for home. After Hiram Galt had said his piece, roping together poles for a play raft for Tad suddenly didn't seem that important.

It was now well into first dark, and Rosie was gasping at the gush of cold running pump water when Jess and Jake Willem rode up.

'If that's you, Jake,' she said, towelling water from her eyes, 'you shouldn't be sitting a horse. And certainly not this one.'

'Nothin' much wrong with my knees, Rosie, or my hands an' arms. An' seein' as I don't do much spurrin' with this one, I can make out.'

Rosie held her hand to the bay's nose, and smiled. 'Hmm, that's as maybe. Are you falling for that maca-roni, Jess?' she asked. 'Or are you just keen to inherit?'

'Ha! Two Jays can't carry a lame duck, Miss Rosie. There's work pilin' up. Wood choppin', raisin' the new barn, ploughin' an' the like,' Jess laughed.

Rosie and Jess watched uneasily as Jake swung down from the saddle, slipped his bad foot from the stirrup. He'd lost a few pounds, had pain around his middle, and was stiff. But he did have the good use of his strong hands and arms.

Self-conscious, he moved his foot awkwardly on the ground. 'It's only pain, an' I got Doc Page's sucky bottle for that,' he said, sensing Rosie's feelings. 'There's some have to live with a lot more'n that.'

It was obvious the man hadn't lost much of his toughness, and Rosie shrugged. 'OK,' she said. 'If you can manage to put your horses into the corral, you can both stay for supper.'

'Where's Tad?' Jess asked.

'Middle of shakedown. Don't wake him.'

After stewed beef and a pile of hot corn, they drank coffee heavily laced with store-bought sugar. When a rider approached at the gallop, it was Jess who first heard it. Jake blew out the lamp before Jess moved a curtain aside.

The Willems had acted so quickly, Rosie realized they were still wearing their guns. Beneath the easy chit-chat, father and son were ready to raise Cain.

'Can you see anythin'?' Jake asked, calmly.

'Yeah, just about. It's the Galt kid, an' I think he's got my mare with him.'

Tyler Galt climbed from his saddle and hitched two horses to a corral post. He had a lingering look at Jake's stallion, then approached the house. 'Rosie . . . Rosie Post,' he called out. 'It's me, Tyler Galt.'

Rosie stepped up to the door and pulled it open. 'Tyler? What's wrong?'

'There's somethin' you got to know.

Roach Tolman brought a stranger from town. It was this afternoon. He said he's . . . '

Tyler stopped as the bright flare of a match suddenly lit the room beyond Rosie. Jake had relighted the lamp, and in its glow, Tyler's face looked tight and worried.

'Come into the house,' Rosie said.

Uneasily, Tyler edged through the doorway. He stared first at Jess, then at Jake who was still holding his coffee can.

'Don't look so troubled, Tyler,' Rosie continued. 'This stranger who came to Bullhead. He said he was a detective from Mitchell. That's what you were going to say, wasn't it?' she said quietly.

Tyler stared at her, confused. 'Yeah, more or less. How'd you know?'

'And how do I know that I'm wanted for murder?' A tiny muscle in the corner of one of Rosie's eyes twitched. 'Because it's true, that's *how*.' She turned to Jake. 'It's the real reason I came to Grip Basin. I shot my sister's husband,' she said.

From Jake's expression, it was clear he was fairly bewildered. 'Is that a good or bad thing?' he asked simply.

Rosie felt weak. She turned and flopped into her fireside rocker, made an indecisive smile. 'Don't fret, Tyler,' she told him. 'Secrets are hardly ever long-lived.' She swallowed hard, her eyes on Jake. She could see the questions in his face.

'Have we all got to get ourselves seated comfortably for this, Rosie?' he asked.

'It might stop you falling over when you hear the bits that you don't know already.'

'Let's hear them bits then,' Jake said.

'Saffy went looking for Derram,' Rosie started to explain. 'I told you he died shortly after Tad was born, but he didn't. He abandoned them . . . left them on the breadline.'

'Why?' Jake asked.

'He didn't want the liability of a wife and child. He was a snake . . . wanted a pit in every town along the Missouri.'

'So you killed him.' Jess was incredulous.

'No. That's not the reason.' Rosie shook her head slowly. 'When our father died, I went to the bank in Pierre. They helped me take care of the sale of the ranch. It was a large sum of money.' Rosie saw the curiosity in Jake's eyes. 'That's when I set out to find Saffy,' she carried on. 'She was living in Pickstown, near the border. There was a lot to tell her about.'

'Half that money was hers though, wasn't it?' Tyler wanted to know.

'For a short while, yes. She'd contracted the typhus. A doctor said it was more than likely caused by a rat flea . . . didn't mention Derram Kale by name.'

Jake gulped at Rosie's righteous anger. 'So, half the estate became young Tad's,' he said.

'No, it didn't. Dad was never going to make provision for a child of Sally's. Not by Derram or anybody else. It all reverted to me.'

'Not a lot the rat flea could do about that, then,' Jess chipped in.

'You wouldn't have thought so. But he didn't see it that way, and got to thinking. He was back, even before I'd got Saffy's burial settled.'

'What did he do?' Tyler pressed, as Rosie's tale unfolded.

Jake and Jess exchanged glances. They both knew Rosie had reached the heart of her story, half-guessed what was coming.

'It was exactly one week after Saffy's death. I was sorting out my and Tad's stuff, getting ready to leave. I wasn't expecting a visit from a black-hearted boatman. He pushed his way in, said he wanted Tad. You'd have thought it was whiskey he was talking about — not his child.'

Rosie continued, her faint caustic smile becoming a grimace. 'I told him 'no, never', that Tad was all the family I had. He lost interest almost immediately, said I was the one he really wanted. He said Saffy had been just a tag on. He said some terrible things about her . . . my sister.'

'So what happened?' Tyler asked eagerly, while Jake just sat and looked.

'I used the derringer dad had given me. In Pickstown, it was what ladies carried in their purses. He came at me and I reeled away . . . pulled the trigger. He was so close. It was all I could . . . ' Rosie shuddered at the horror of the memory.

'Where was Tad?' Tyler went on with his questioning.

'Yeah, an' how'd you get away?' Jess asked quickly.

'Tad was there. He was with me . . . standing, watching and listening. I grabbed him and the bag I'd been packing. We ran out onto the the fire escape, down the steps. I had *some* money on account at the town bank. We got to Chamberlain and caught the stage west. Stayed in Draper and Belvidere, never far off the coach route. Then we headed on through the

Badlands to Rapid City.'

There was an uneasy silence and Rosie gave Jake a weak smile. 'We stayed there a few weeks,' she said. 'I didn't know what to do . . . where to go next. I could hardly raise a smile from Tad. I thought of giving myself up. Tad would have been all right. It isn't as though he'd always be penniless.'

'How'd you figure that?' Jess asked. Jake continued with his looking.

'I made out a trust fund.'

'How old's he have to be before he collects?' Tyler was keen to know.

'Half at sixteen. The balance on majority.'

'You reckon it's all fate, Rosie?' Jake eventually asked.

Rosie thought for a moment before answering. Then she looked at Jake wistfully. 'If fate was a Rapid City bank manager telling me he knew of a small ranch for sale, then yes, I guess so. After all, I'm here with Tad *and* the money.'

'Yeah, well, most places have a Derram Kale, Rosie. An' Grip Basin's no exception. Anyone who lives under the influence of . . . ' Jake stopped, turned to Tyler. 'It's gettin' dark, Tyler, an' maybe time you took to the saddle. Our talk ain't goin' to get too neighbourly. It's likely to get close to HOG.'

Tyler coloured a little. 'I've already heard things,' he said. 'That's why I came to tell Rosie what I did. An' there's a big moon risin'.'

14

Staying Home

'Yeah, so there is, Tyler. It's just that Pa don't want any unnecessary trouble over you,' Jess said, in response to Tyler Galt's chiding. 'So, stay for a while an' tell us about that detective. How'd you reckon he got in tow with Tolman?'

'They must have been in the White Glass. I think his name was Boone. He said he'd been told in Rapid City that Pa could help him find the person he was after.'

'When?' Jess asked.

'Er. When was what?'

'When they met up?'

'Not sure. They rode home about noon. I was in the house, but they didn't know it. I thought it was Pa with Roach, so I kept quiet.'

'Smart move,' Jess muttered.

'Yeah, they're both a bit scratchy. Roach would have skinned me if he knew I was there . . . still might.'

Jake shook his head and smiled reassuringly. 'Why'd you think this detective was spillin' the beans to Tolman?'

'Roach said he'd shoot his face off, unless he got a name. He would've too. I think he said Miss Rosie wouldn't get taken away.'

Rosie looked unbelievingly at Tyler. 'Are you sure you heard right?' she asked.

'What the hell's goin' on here, Pa . . . Rosie? I'm sort o' lost,' Jess huffed.

'Tyler?' Jake said, implying that Tyler should continue.

'Roach said he'd get the boy . . . Tad. The detective was goin' back to Mitchell to report Rosie dead.'

'Why the hell would he do that?' Jess started again.

'Blackmail. Tolman knows I'll stay if he's got Tad,' Rosie explained without hesitation.

'You can't argue with his reasonin'. It's his means to an end, I guess,' Jake said. 'Anythin' else, Tyler?'

'I saw 'em together in the yard. Roach got a wagon harnessed an' loaded up with boxes an' salt sacks. He told some of the boys he was goin' stock fishin'. But he ain't. He's just keepin' well clear o' Pa.'

'That's the lot then is it, Tyler?' Jess asked him.

Tyler shook his head. 'No, not quite. Roach said he wanted the bay. Before he left he gave Fole Stiller some money. Told him to stay behind and keep tabs on Mr Willem, Jess an' Rosie.'

'How did you say you know all this, Tyler?' from Rosie. 'How did you hear it?'

'From the top o' the staircase outside o' my room. Then they were in the yard. Pa weren't around, so there was no need for Roach to keep quiet about anythin'.'

'Yeah, fair enough, kid,' Jake said, his mind turning suddenly to something else. 'Could Stiller have followed you here?'

Tyler shook his head again. 'I don't think so. Why'd he want to do that?' Tyler moved uncertainly towards the door. 'I've got to tell Pa,' he said. 'He don't know all of what's goin' on.'

'That's not quite what he told *me*,' Rosie muttered, tiredly. But she liked the youngster's openness and his sense of an injustice being done. 'It's good that you've done this, Tyler. I know . . . we *all* know it's not easy. But don't go against your pa . . . no matter what,' she said kindly.

'Yeah, you done just fine, just fine,' Jake added. 'There's nothin' goin' to happen to Rosie or the little 'un. Much of it, down to you.'

Tyler grinned manfully. 'I saw the bay when I came in. Do you think I could ride him sometime?' he asked.

'Yeah, I'm sure he'd like that. He ain't that much older'n you,' Jake said and winked.

'I'll ride out to the wagon road with

Tyler. Get me a good look at that big old moon,' Jess said.

★ ★ ★

A while later, Rosie looked up from her rocker. 'I hope that boy's not headed for a wasted life. He's not getting much of a start in Grip Basin,' she said to Jake.

'It won't be wasted if he learns from it.'

'No, I guess not. He's maybe seen Roach Tolman for what he is, so that's *good*. But he's rode off hoping his big ox pa's going to put everything to rights, and that's *bad*.'

'Yeah. That's sort o' what I meant, Rosie,' Jake said slow and uncertainly.

The two of them then sat for a while in silence. They listened to night sounds, the occasional sleepy gasps from Tad's converted wood store that led off the back corner of the room.

Rosie's mind was drifting with wretched thoughts about Derram Kale, bigoted juries and 'guilty' verdicts.

'I don't want to be hunted down, Jake. I want to be like ordinary folk — sit on the stoop an' read the wish book, shuck peas, go to Sunday prayers.'

'It's a fact I ain't ever had the first part, Rosie, but I've sure wanted to be peaceable. Don't seem possible if you got a pretty neighbour, a blood mount an' a firebrand son.'

They both laughed quietly. Then Jake asked Rosie what she was going to do.

'Throw myself at the mercy of Mitchell's court. Or off a rocky mountain,' she added wryly.

'No. Both o' them are out. There's a third way,' Jake said slowly, as if weighing up the options. 'No one, an' I mean *no one*, wants you to leave here, Rosie. We all kind o' like havin' you around. I reckon we'd miss you . . . not least, ol' Tadskins there.'

'And the fighting would still go on,' Rosie furthered.

Jake grinned. 'Yeah, o' course it

would. As long as there's mirrors, Stiller ain't goin' to forget what Jess did to him. Tolman an' me ain't exactly that close, an' then there's the bay.'

'And because of *me*, we can't bring in the law?'

'We can't anyway, Rosie. You heard Tyler say that Stiller was being paid to watch us. Well, think about it. Tolman wouldn't be ridin' off, if he thought we'd leave the basin to find outside help.' Jake limped to the window, stared into the night. 'Who'd ever have thought we'd be fightin' to get *away* from here.'

'It must be a real ill wind that blows off those hills,' Rosie murmured sadly.

Jake smiled suddenly. 'Get used to it, Rosie, you're stayin' home. An' you don't need *me* to tell you that it ain't for the satisfaction o' Roach Tolman.'

'I can't believe that men are prepared to fight — to use guns, over things like this,' she said, in an incredulous whisper.

'Good God, Rosie. Out here, women

an' horses are the *only* things they fight over. They'll even wager on the outcomes, an' fight over *that*.'

Rosie dragged her fingers slowly through her hair. 'If it's not that man Boone who comes after me, it'll be someone else. Nothing's going to change that, Jake.'

'Nothin' to date,' he agreed, then winced as a twist of pain ran through his foot. 'But you *can* afford some big-shot attorney.'

Rosie accepted Jake's humour but didn't smile. 'I'm sorry I lied to you, Jake . . . real sorry,' she said. 'I guess I didn't want my life to sound so dreadful . . . was tired of being on my own . . . only Tad.'

Jake reached to the table for his makings. 'I already said, you ain't on your own, Rosie,' he said after a few seconds. 'An' we'll be gettin' us some company, real soon.'

Rosie closed her eyes at the thought. 'I was forgetting,' she said. 'The *third* way, you mentioned.'

15

The Bobtail

When Jess and Tyler got to the wagon road, they circuited back through the trees. Jess said it was for the sake of his own hide to see no harm came to Tyler. They came in from the west of HOG, where timber would screen them from the bunkhouse and the moonlight vigilance of Fole Stiller.

If Tolman's top hand caught sight of Tyler, he'd guess where he'd been and progress trouble. Whereas Tyler wanted to see his father and tell him the truth, ask him to withdraw from it.

A half-mile from the ranch house they reined in to the cottonwood stand.

'You don't have to come no further, Jess,' Tyler said. 'Stiller ain't around . . . can't see much else.'

'Don't mean to say there's no one

there, kid,' Jess was doubtful. 'My pa said nothin' was goin' to harm you . . . more or less.'

Tyler thought for a moment. 'Well, mine might start to rattle. But if he listens to me, he won't bite. I'll be all right, Jess.'

'Well, OK. I'll just sit for a while an' jaw with these cottonwoods . . . ask 'em if they know of a good party comin' up.'

Outside of the house's lamp-lights, Tyler shuddered at the thought of Jess's quip. He had to force himself to face his father. The old man had warned him about going anywhere near Two Jays. And if he knew what Roach had been up to behind his back, Jess would maybe get his answer from the cotton-woods.

But having told Rosie and Jake what he was going to do, Tyler wasn't about to break his word. Unseen, he dis-mounted and walked his horse to the barn. It was almost black dark inside, but he managed to unsaddle. He had a glance around him, then ran around the front of the house, hoping that Husky — who usually took himself a late foot watch — had turned in.

For a full minute, Tyler crouched beneath a side window, listening. Then he went around to the back of the house, let himself in through a narrow door that opened into the pantry store-room. He listened again, before edging into the kitchen proper.

Lights from the main room filtered through the house, and he gulped air, as Grif Earnley suddenly walked within three paces of him. He swallowed, then cursed under his breath as the kitchen door slammed to.

Tyler wondered what his father's old-time friend had been doing there. Grif Earnley had always been a star-pitch cowboy, didn't often come into the house.

Tyler sensed trouble cloying at the night air. He was almost breathless as he walked into the spacious, ash-panelled HOG parlour.

'Hello, Pa,' he said, the tremble from

his knees spreading up through his body.

With his feet out on a buffalo-head stool, Hiram Galt was sitting in a wing chair. Between his big fingers, he held an empty whiskey glass. His head was pitched forward, his jowels resting heavy on his chest. At the sound of Tyler's voice he snorted and looked up slowly, held his young son with shrewd eyes. 'You ought to be more careful, boy,' he rumbled. 'It's a sorry bird that fouls its own nest.'

It took a moment for Tyler to understand. 'You got Grif watchin' me,' he said, aware that Stiller was doing exactly the same for Roach Tolman.

'Watchin' *over* you, Tyler. Besides, a man in my position needs more'n one set of eyes an' ears.'

'Well none of 'em are much use to you,' Tyler hollered back. 'You got no feelin' for folk. You're doin' wrong an' you ain't bothered.'

Galt dropped his glass, pounded his fist against his knee. 'Goddamnit, Tyler, you don't talk to me like that,' he raged. 'Not in this house.'

But Tyler forged ahead. 'What do you mean, *this house*?' he shouted back. 'It should be *our house*, Pa.' Tyler's voice was shaky, but he blinked hard and carried on. 'All them eyes an' ears are no good if . . . no good if . . . ' There was so much welling up inside Tyler, that suddenly he wanted to get away — get some of Grif Earnley's weather in his face. 'Roach murdered Tom Owers, an' nothin' happened. That was 'cause o' you.'

Galt went stiff with anger then he swung off his chair. He looked as though he was ready to horn the walls.

'You got here first, Pa, an' you're the biggest an' the most powerful. But you don't own the whole basin. Rosie Post, an' Jake an' Jess Willem ain't goin' to roll over. They own that land along Oglala Creek, right and proper, an' they're goin' to stand up to you. You got to ease up, Pa. You ain't no spike buck any longer . . . God neither,' Tyler hit him with, as he backed off.

'Your new buddies got 'emselves a mail man, have they?' Galt rasped derisively. 'Well, you gone an' delivered, Tyler. Now stuff a bindle an' get out.'

Tyler shook his head sadly. 'I ain't come to deliver anything, Pa,' he stated. 'Up until a moment ago, I lived here, remember? But there's just one thing else, I think you should know about Roach. He's goin' — '

'I said, *get out*, you goddamn little squealer. You've said your piece,' Galt barked, as he moved forward heavily.

Tyler hadn't the wrath or bitter words his father lashed him with, but he'd got the Galt spirit, and for a moment he held his father's challenging gaze. Then, with an accommodating smile he shrugged, turned on his heel and left the house.

In the cool night air he swore, looked towards the distant cottonwood stand, and hoped that Jess was still out there. Then he eyed a well-muscled roan, that was nosing its way around the corral. 'My goin' away present,' he muttered.

* * *

Tyler was trembling with excitement when, once again, he drew near to the Catkin ranch. It was close to daybreak, but there was a light still burning.

'I saw that happen before,' he said, and laughed when the yellow glow suddenly turned to darkness.

'What was that?' Jess asked.

'Someone dampin' down the lamp.'

Tyler was right. From inside the house, Jake eased down the hammer of Rosie's Winchester. 'Jess's back,' he said. 'But it looks like young Tyler's still with him.'

Rosie quickly relit the lamp. 'Tyler?' she questioned. 'I wonder what's happened?'

'For the time taken, they could've both ridden to Deadwood an' back.'

'Don't shoot,' Jess shouted, as he pushed at the door. 'Me an' Trooper

Tyler Galt come in peace.'

Jess and Tyler were also exhausted. Tyler was slurring his words, falling asleep as he related the night time's events.

When he'd finished, Jake sat very quietly, taking it all in. He knew that what Rosie had said about Tyler going against his pa was right. Although it sounded like Hiram Galt hadn't cut his son much slack.

And Rosie had similar thoughts, when she broke the silence. 'You surprised him by growing up,' she said. 'Raising's different from letting grow. I think your pa's just found that out. He'll ease up.'

Tyler rubbed his eyes and yawned. 'Naah. Real HOG men ain't long on mercy.' He smiled wearily. 'If you could, Miss . . . Rosie. I'd be grateful for a night's — '

'You can make up a pallet in the barn. There's just about room.'

Jess grinned at Tyler. 'Welcome, Bobtail,' he said tiredly. 'Welcome to the 1st Oglala Creek Rag-Tag Resistance.'

16

Laying the Odds

Halfway through the following morning, Grif Earnley rode up to the HOG main house on a sweat-flecked horse.

'He went straight to the Catkin spread,' he reported, as Hiram Galt stepped onto the broad terrace. 'That young Willem was waitin' for him by the cottonwoods. That'll be four of 'em out there now.'

Galt groped for a suitable oath, brought to mind a likeness of Rosie Post. His thick knuckles turned bone white as he gripped the handrail of the balcony. He could have dealt with the Willems if it hadn't have been for her. She was a handsome woman, and he understood the consequences of her arrival. She was the bolt of lightning that *did* strike twice, as far as Jake

Willem and Roach Tolman were concerned.

It was after refusing his offer for the Catkin, that Galt decided Rosie's stint at ranching was up. At the time, he thought he'd leave her to Tolman, but now *he'd* have to step in, before he lost any more control of his supposed allies.

'Find Husky,' he said sullenly. 'Then come on in. I'll get us some table fixins'.'

As they forked up fried potatoes, eggs and chicken, Galt searched the men's faces for signs of waywardness. 'We won't be hearin' much from Two Jays after tomorrow,' he asserted. 'An' as for the maverick? Well, he ain't goin' to change my plans much. He's runnin bad, an' you boys got to remember that, when time's up.'

Galt knew they wouldn't like his stance, or his planned assault on Catkin. Grif Earnley would always have an obligation to Tyler's welfare, but he said nothing.

The sun was very high when Husky brought out Galt's rig. As he backed up the mare, he called for Galt to look west. The stock wagon, with two men up, was approaching and Galt immediately recognized Roach Tolman as the driver.

He spat into the ground. 'If it ain't tied down, it comes back,' he muttered to himself. Galt's blood raced, as he thought of Tolman's pursuit of Rosie Post, the stupidity of his getting Stiller to shoot up Jake Willem. That was the reason for the girl throwing in with them, partly to blame for young Tyler leaving, too.

He stepped away from the rig, took a deep breath and clenched his fists. As the wagon pulled into the yard, he threw a blank look at the Missouri River detective, then took a menacing step forward as Tolman climbed down.

'Where the hell you been?' he asked abruptly.

Tolman looked wary and uncomfortable. 'Stock ponds. Got tired of eatin' goddamn cow meat. Fish must be off o' their feed though . . . ' Seeing the explanation was going nowhere with Galt, the foreman stopped. He looked at the detective, back to Galt. 'This is Henry Boone. He's — '

Galt cut in. 'How long's it been since you stopped takin' my orders, Roach, an' started lyin' instead? An' I thought I said to stay away 'til you got word.'

Tolman stared angrily at Galt. Then he calmed down a bit. 'You got your wants an' wishes, boss, well, I got mine. Same coin . . . differin' sides. But you probably got somethin' else bitin' your ass. I hear Tyler's up an' flown the nest.'

Momentarily, Galt accepted the daring raillery, knew it was for the benefit of the man called Boone. 'Yeah, looks like he's decided to ride with the Willems and the Post woman.' He looked icily at Tolman. 'Let's hope it's only fly an' ointment stuff, Roach, 'cause it was *you* taught him how to shoot.'

'What do you mean by that?'

'You're takin' a passel o' blame for this family rift. An' you'll pay for it, if anythin' happens to Tyler. Sure the kid's messed up by goin' over to Catkin, but you've rode bell on it, Roach. Now I've made up my mind. They all got one more day along that creek, then they go. Boots on or off, it's up to them.'

Tolman made a slight, twisted grin. 'I wouldn't appreciate you doin' that, boss. I ain't the draw off o' this outfit, an' I'm takin' care o' the Catkin filly.'

Husky had hitched up the rig mare. He held on to the traces, and muttered something, shook his head at the inevitable.

'Ha. If you ever get to tellin' *her* that, Roach, make sure Jake Willem ain't around. Next time he might not be so gentle, if it's Rosie Post you're fightin' over.'

The two men were glaring at each

other defiantly. Boone remained seated on the wagon. Like Husky, he, too, had sensed that Galt was a man tired of talking.

Galt's voice growled on into the quietness. 'Willem will see you dead, if you chase that girl. An' *me* if you go up against HOG. Them's bad odds, Roach.'

Tolman pushed a knuckle across his mouth while he thought. 'Then somehow I'll have to even 'em up,' he said, with a shade of warning.

In flashing a mutual look with Boone, Tolman was too late to avoid Galt's fist. With brutal speed, the big ham was up and striking under his jaw with the force of a piston. His legs didn't have time to buckle, he went to the ground straight, and lay there unmoving.

For the first time in many weeks, Hiram Galt gave a satisfied smile. 'That's the ground I walk on,' he said, but didn't give Tolman another look. He glared at Boone. 'I don't know who the hell you are, mister, but you're on my property,' he told him, adjusting the rake of his Stetson. 'So get off my goddamn wagon, an' find whatever it was you rode in here on. If Tolman comes to before you're gone, drag him away with you.'

Galt nodded once at Husky as he climbed into his rig. He flicked the reins and the claybank responded. He was headed for Catkin, and dust billowed as he careened from the yard onto the wagon road.

17

Standing Fast

It wasn't only to protect Rosie Post and Tad Raster that the Willems stayed on at Catkin. On all sides of the ranch house, flat grass land stretched for nearly a mile. According to Tyler Galt, Roach Tolman was coming, so they chose it for its defensive capability. No one knew if Tolman had any back up, but Tyler said he'd heard Tolman tell Boone that a few broke cowboys had been paid fighting wages to join up with him.

Jake made the tactical decisions. When the attack came, he'd take the front. Tyler and Jess would look out to the east and south, where the angle of view also covered some land to their blind-sided north. Together, they'd hold a position that would be difficult to over-run. From the trees was a distance beyond the exacting range of a rifle bullet, and better than Two Jays, where the timber-line closed up on the house and its outbuildings.

In the pearly light of daybreak, Tyler reminded Jake that Tolman was still hell-bent on getting the bay. 'Anyone would want a horse like that,' he said. 'Difference is, Roach usually gets what he wants.' Tyler looked into Jake's tough, uncompromising face. 'Well up to *now*, that is,' he added hastily. 'But now you're an *enemy* as well. You know . . . anyone else that's fightin' *you* . . . he'll get them in a gather. He gets the right sidin'. That's why Stiller's out for Jess. Roach's been ridin' him for the revenge.'

Jake looked towards his son. 'What your gran'pa said about this land bein' sweet, was right enough, Jess. But he sure got it wrong about some o' its citizens,' he said thoughtfully.

Tyler was still considering his own involvement, being squared off with

Roach Tolman, his pa, the stand-fast at Catkin. He peered out of the window beside Jess. 'I guess Pa's madder at Roach than he is with me,' he continued dismally. 'I told him what was happenin' . . . what I was doin'. Roach never did. *That's* what Pa don't like.'

'That's the impression I got about your pa, Tyler,' Rosie agreed. 'He thinks that knowing everything is his strength. But it's become his weakness.'

Jake listened, thought for a second. 'Yeah, you're right. This has turned into who's lead steer. Just supposin' your pa an' Tolman got to lockin' their horns over all this, Tyler,' he said. 'You say Tolman's got his own men, but who'd the HOG boys follow?'

'They wouldn't fight Pa. Some of 'em been on HOG a long time. Stiller's the only one who'd go along with Roach.'

Jake's eyes narrowed. 'Then maybe that's all we need . . . what we can hope for. Divide an' conquer,' he said, with a short, sharp smile.

'Don't forget Tolman's Missouri detective,' Jess chipped in. 'We'll more'n likely be swappin' lead with him.'

'I haven't forgot him, Jess. I ain't goin' to forget anyone who's capable o' doin' that. Which reminds me: we ought to get over to Two Jays,' he said. 'Let Edson know what we're doin.' He can have a look at my foot, while you load the wagon. I want us well armed.'

Jess nodded. Rosie and Tyler smiled uncertainly.

★   ★   ★

After they had gone, time dragged as Rosie tended to small, routine chores. She had to give Tad more play space than the house provided, and it was difficult to keep an eye on him when he wanted to explore beyond the stoop. But since they'd first met in the Twist Wind hotel, Tyler had taken to the toddler. As far as Tad was concerned, Tyler had no less natural caring ability than Rosie had, and that meant she could ride line around the near-to-home pasture.

That was when she remembered the run of broken fencing she'd seen when returning from the creek with Tad. She wasn't in a particular mending frame of mind, and wouldn't have need of a wire cutter or hammer and staples, but she was duty-bound to carry the Winchester.

She went to the small corral and saddled her chestnut cow pony. There could be little danger involved in such a short ride. She was only going to check it out, and she told Tyler as much. She told him to stay near the house, keep an eye on Tad. 'It's not far. Stand on tiptoe and you'll probably see me,' she said. 'And I won't be that long, either. Be back before your belly gets to rumble.'

Nevertheless, not wanting to be surprised or trapped, Rosie did begin to worry, wondered from what direction Tolman and his henchmen would show. It was in keeping a watchful eye that she saw Hiram Galt approaching. From half a mile away, there was no mistaking the big rancher. He was, as usual, dressed dark, and yanking at the reins of the rig mare. He was riding hard along the fence line, and Rosie had a nervous glance at the distance that separated them. She pulled the Winchester, took a longer look and levered a shell into the breech.

It didn't look like a major assault, or was Galt ahead of Tolman? A squaring off with his son, maybe? Rosie gave a wry smile. Whichever, Catkin land was certainly one of his favoured meeting places.

Then Rosie saw the other riders. There were two of them, and they were a way behind. Unaware of the chase, Galt just came riding on, making straight for Rosie.

She turned the pony side on and levelled the Winchester. As Galt approached, she felt immediately more nervous as the two back riders suddenly peeled away.

They rode to the east, and in a brief,

uneasy flash it occurred to Rosie that none of them could have known they'd meet her, or anyone else, away from the house.

She looked into Galt's icy stare, felt his dark eyes estimating her mood as he closed in. His mare was snorting, and its neck and shoulders were splashed with gobbets of sweaty froth. The cloth of Galt's coat was dirt-scuffed, and with a tear in the knee of a trouser leg, Rosie notioned he'd taken a fall.

And that was true. Galt had lost control as he'd veered off the wagon road. He'd turned the rig and been thrown, but he'd rolled with it, and apart from shaking himself up a bit, only got some body bruising. It had cost him no more than the time it took the pursuing Tolman and Henry Boone to get within a few hundred yards of him.

Rosie flinched from the man's livid features, his cramped anger as he leaned towards her.

'It'll take more'n you an' that pretty

smoke pole to stop me, lady,' Galt snarled, using brute strength to control the agitated mare. 'I'll use it to . . . '

Galt's threat trailed off in choked anger as he kicked and jerked the rig forward. Rosie's pony shied away, its eyes bulging with panic.

Rosie didn't know what it was that Galt wanted, couldn't understand why, with his rage, he didn't pull a gun. She swung up the rifle. 'You're on my land,' she yelled, cursing immediately at the futility.

She whirled her pony away, turned and fired a single shot high above the rig. Galt's mare reared in its traces, threw its hips sideways. Rosie kicked her heels and fired again. It was all she could do, other than shoot the man as he dragged desperately on the reins. Momentarily, the Pickstown room swam into Rosie's thoughts, then she yelled for the chestnut to run.

At the thought of Galt chasing her home, anger suddenly flared in Rosie. She pulled at the reins, kept up the pressure until they came to a standstill. She jumped down and kneeled while the chestnut walked off a few paces.

'Damn you, Hiram Galt,' she muttered from her parched mouth. 'You're not getting any nearer those boys.' Her heart thumped uncontrollably as she saw Galt gaining ground. She turned once and looked back towards the house, rebuked herself for leaving Tad and Tyler on their own. She hoped they'd make themselves safe inside the house, that Jake and Jess would be returning from Two Jays. But that was a forlorn hope. It was too soon. With the freighter even partly loaded, they'd have to take the wagon road.

'You're not one for choices, are you?' she uttered. Then she aimed and pulled the trigger. It was a good shot from a narrow angle, and she saw Galt gasp as the bullet thumped into the high part of his leg. But nothing more happened. The mare faltered once, slewed, and Galt urged it on.

'I'll take your head right off. I can do

it,' Rosie yelled. She could see the tearing rage across Galt's face, the anticipation of more pain as her next bullet ripped into the seat beside him. She used some rivermen's language that she'd learned from her sister. It was the angry, desperation brand that came as the typhus had gripped her.

Rosie took one, then two sideways steps and aimed for Galt's chest, held it steady while he advanced. He was so close, she could hear him.

'You must have some snake in you,' Galt rasped. 'You shootin' me in cold blood.' He took off his hat, breathed deep and painful. As the rig mare stepped ever closer, Rosie increased her finger pressure on the trigger. But she didn't fire. She listened, was gripped with Galt's words, the memory of Derram Kale.

'You know I want you out o' the basin.' Galt managed an evil grimace. 'Acceptin' we ain't ever goin' to be partners, that ain't too much to ask, is it? An' I could get real irritated at you

140

puttin' bullets in me.' His words ended with a snorting laugh.

'You'll never get beyond *irritated*, Mr Galt. Please don't make me shoot again.' Rosie's breathing was fast and shallow. She reminded herself that Galt was Tyler's father.

The silence was overpowering. Within moments, grasshoppers flicked back to within inches of where Rosie knelt. Other than the two mounts snorting nervous exchanges, they made the only sounds.

Rosie was silently reciting, merging prayers with cuss words, when the man's chest exploded. It was almost simultaneous with the crash of the rifle shot from behind her. She watched spellbound, riveted with fear as Galt fell forward. He coughed and raised his head, dropped the reins. His enormous hands opened and closed and he stared without focus. His last words were low and heavy.

'You're somethin' else, lady.'

The man grunted, heaved his big

shoulders and buckled down from the rig seat. He hit the ground with a dull thud as Rosie got to her feet. She turned to the south, just glimpsed a horse cantering beyond the fence line. The rider was crouched low, but familiar as he kicked his horse for the line of timber.

Rosie looked towards the house, saw Tyler already racing through the pasture towards her. He *had* been keeping a look out, would have heard the shooting, maybe seen it. But it wasn't the way it looked.

She walked quickly towards her pony, rammed the rifle back in its holster. Then, with more cursing, she went back to Galt's body, waited to face the torment of his young son.

18

Call for Help

As the first crack of Rosie's Winchester echoed across the home pasture, Tyler quickly pushed Tad under his cot. He grabbed his own gun and rushed for the door. He stopped, was standing with his back to it, breathing fast, when he heard the second shot. Then he quickly jumped to the outside, his eyes searching for movement. He saw it, gasped with relief when he saw his father riding steadily towards Rosie. They were almost midway between the yard gate and the fence line, but even from that distance, Tyler could see that Galt's advance on Rosie was threatening.

He called out and waved his arms when he saw Rosie dismount and kneel. He pushed the door hard against the latch, was running swift and reckless when the next shots came. He yelled frantically when he saw his pa crumple from the rig and fall to the ground.

He ran on, staggered to where his father lay. He stared down, his lungs heaving. 'I saw. You shot him, Rosie. You — '

Rosie let go of her rifle held out her hands. 'I . . . I *didn't* shoot him, Tyler,' she faltered back. 'I didn't fire . . . not that last one.'

The two stared hard at each other.

'He's dead,' Tyler said heavily.

'Yes . . . but . . . ' Rosie gulped. 'He rode at me. Why? What have I done?'

'I saw you shootin' him. That's what you were doin'. Don't you know?'

Rosie was shaking. 'That was to stop him, Tyler. I hit him in the leg. There was another shot . . . after. There was someone else.'

Tyler looked towards the fence line, where it cornered at the edge of the trees. Then he turned back to Rosie. 'I guess whoever it was, ain't there anymore,' he said accusingly.

'Where's Tad? What did you do with him?' Rosie asked, suddenly frightened again.

'He's safe inside.'

But Rosie was hardly listening, she was staring back at the timberline. She knew there'd been a killer somewhere in the trees, who was maybe still there. 'We've got to get back . . . got to take your pa.' she said, trying to hide her fright.

They both had tears running down their faces, found breathing difficult as they lifted Galt from the blood-soaked grass, as they dragged the deadweight body up and across the seat of the rig.

It was another fifteeeen minutes before they stumbled their way back to the house. Tyler had been thinking, getting a grip on what he'd seen and heard. 'Reckon I did see you lookin', Rosie,' he said, as they went through the gate into the yard. 'After that last shot, you looked behind you.'

'I know, I told you, Tyler. But it's of

no help. Whoever killed your pa's running the blame on me. That was their plan. I can't prove I didn't kill him, and what you saw can only muddy the waters.'

Tyler wanted to forget it, but deep down, he knew that Rosie was telling the truth. 'No, it's *them*, Rosie. *They* have to prove you killed him. I know that, 'cause it's what Pa was always usin' for his defence. So they can't do it. 'Specially if I bend the truth about what I saw. An' that's somethin' else Pa said. The law's meant to be *lenient*. Sometimes it *leans* one way . . . sometimes another.'

Rosie shook her head despairingly, then calling for Tad, she dismounted and ran for the front door. Tyler's mind was also racing with uncertainty and jumbled emotions. He knew that with his pa dead, Roach Tolman would be the walking boss of Grip Basin, regardless of HOG Ranch or who owned it.

'I'm going after Jake and Jess,' Rosie

said, as soon as she'd made sure Tad was safe, after they'd manhandled Galt's body into the draped nook of Rosie's bedroom. 'Remember, it's *me* they want. So stay inside with Tad and keep the doors shut. You'll be safe enough.'

★   ★   ★

For a long while, Tyler sat staring at his dark-bloodied father, the ashen, grizzled face. He held on to a carved puppet, mindlessly banged it up and down on the floor as Tad responded to the noisy repetition.

'You do blubbin' as well, Tyler?' the child asked solemnly.

'No. As well as *who*?'

'The man,' the child said, pointing at Galt's body.

Tyler grinned sadly. 'That's . . . that's because *he ain't dead*,' he gasped, leaping to his feet when his father emitted a low sigh.

Feeling queasy and very lonely, Tyler

cut away the sticky torn suiting, then looked around for cloths and water. His pa had the constitution of a grizzly, but Tyler was dumbfounded, flinched when the big, tough rancher's eyes flickered. He was swallowing hard, making an attempt to clean the chest wound when he heard the sound of the rear door being opened. He groaned wretchedly, reached out and pulled Tad towards him. He stood silent and looked round the room for his rifle, remembered he'd left it on the boot box, out front.

'You shoulda locked *all* the doors, kid,' Tolman snarled, as he stepped into the room with Henry Boone. 'Where's Rosie Post?'

'Stiller told you we were here. You paid him to keep watch on us. I heard you,' Tyler charged.

'You heard me, you say?' Tolman took a threatening step forward.

Tyler was suddenly fearful. With his defiant, raw anger, he'd trapped himself. 'I was in the house when you came in with *him*,' he said, nodding towards

Boone. 'I heard everythin' you said about Rosie.'

Tolman rubbed his chin, looked dangerous. 'I asked you where she was?' he snarled again.

'You find out. Ask Stiller, why don't you?' Tyler replied doggedly.

Tolman's eyes moved around the room. 'No need,' he said, seeing Galt's body partly screened on the bed behind Tyler. 'She *was* here. She helped you get your pa back, after shootin' him.'

'You know she was shootin' at Pa?' Tyler asked. 'How? How'd you know?'

As Tolman was thinking about his response, Boone cut in. 'We saw. It was from a distance, but we saw her. She shot him dead, no mistake.'

Tyler shuffled sideways. He wanted to draw their attention away from the bed, hoped his pa didn't make another noise. 'She fired to stop him, not kill him,' he said. 'If you'd been HOG side, you'd know . . . unless . . . ' Tyler stopped, looked quickly from Boone to Tolman.

'Steady on, kid. You're a little mixed up . . . ain't exactly a reliable witness. We know what we saw,' Boone said. He waited while Tyler thought about what he was saying, then, while Tolman cast another glance at Galt, he continued, 'Smokin' fellers ain't a problem for Rosie Post, or should I say, for Martha Swann. It don't matter whether they're innocent or guilty. She's actin' judge, jury an' executioner. The little 'un here' — he gestured towards Tad — 'he's her nephew all right, but his last name's Kale, not Raster. She shot his father in cold blood . . . from real close up.' Then Boone looked smugly at Tyler. 'That sound familiar to you, kid?'

Tyler's chest was heaving, and he was shaking his head wearily. As though he sensed the deadlock, Tad stood in the middle of the room looking up at the faces.

Tyler badly wanted Rosie to return with Jess and Jake. 'No!' he burst out. 'You were in the house . . . I heard it all . . . what you were goin' to do.'

150

Tolman laughed. 'You been brought up to hear, see an' be silent, Tyler. But I sure wish I'd known you were there, eavesdroppin'.'

Boone had been thinking on what Tyler had just said. 'Then she knows I'm here in Bullhead?' he demanded.

'Yeah, Rosie knows. So do Jess an' Jake. They're on the way back here an' — '

' — an' we'll be waitin' for 'em. That's the nub of it, kid,' Tolman sneered quickly at Tyler's warning.

As they exchanged their fighting talk, Tyler strained his ears for the slightest sound of horses in the yard. He'd so wanted to prove himself worthy, to defend what was right and proper with Rosie and the Willems. But now it seemed he'd wholly failed them.

Boone seemed to sense Tyler's thoughts and he stepped to one side, looked sidelong through the front window. 'We're riskin' a lot by stayin' here, Roach,' he said. 'Remember what I told you about this little feller an' his

151

share o' the Swann boat business? Well, I'm thinkin' there's Derram Kale's old folk as well. Maybe we'll inherit from both sides. So why don't we go now? We've had our day.'

'The sun ain't fully dipped yet,' Tolman said, looking hard and quick at the detective. 'An' I ain't got *all* I want from Grip Basin,' he added threateningly.

Tyler thought he knew what Tolman meant. 'If that's so, you ain't goin' anywhere, Roach,' he insisted. 'Besides, Rosie says she'll follow you all the way to hell, if anythin' happens to Tad.'

'To hell, eh?' Tolman echoed with mock awe. 'Would sure make an interestin' ride.'

Clutching firmly at Tad, Tyler backed off. The child felt the nervous grip around his shoulders and whimpered.

'Quit squealin',' Tolman threatened, as he crowded them against the far wall of the room.

Tyler twisted himself in front of Tad. 'Go on, Roach, do it,' he dared. 'But you'll have to kill us both. If we're left to tell about what you did here, you'll never be puttin' another foot in the Dakotas . . . be as good as dead.'

'You think you're as smart as your old man, do you?' Tolman snorted, then lashed out with the flat of his hand.

The blow caught Tyler solidly across the side of his face. His head seemed to explode and Tolman socked him again. He blinked against the shock, fought the flashing lights of pain.

Tad gave a muffled cry and Tyler wanted to protect and fight for him. But there wasn't time, and he lashed out with a futile punch. As he closed his eyes, he thought he called for his pa, didn't know whether anyone heard him or not.

19

Enemies Within

When Rosie rode in to Two Jays, Jake was watching Jess as he hefted a sack of tinned foodstuffs onto the freighter.

'What's happened?' he yelled, seeing the dark, sweaty sheen along the flanks of Rosie's pony.

'Hiram Galt's been shot. He's dead.' Barely pausing to catch breath, Rosie told of the shooting. 'But Tyler only knows half the truth,' she concluded. 'I saw and recognized the rider. It was the man who shot his pa, and I didn't . . . couldn't tell him.'

'Roach Tolman,' Jake and Jess said forcefully and almost in unison.

'That's right. One of Tyler's boyhood champions.' Rosie remained sitting her pony. She looked tired and distressed.

'Well, I guess we have to do

somethin' about that,' Jess said anxiously. 'And fast, if Tyler's alone there with Tad . . . again,' he furthered as a murmur, but Rosie heard him.

'Jess is right. We'll leave the wagon . . . just take bullets, an' I'll grab me some of Ed's physic,' Jake glanced at Rosie. 'We can't have you fightin' murder charges right across the State, can we?' he said. 'An' somehow, we've got to get through to the sheriff's office . . . let 'em know what the hell's goin' on here.'

★   ★   ★

The three riders slowed to a canter then Jake pulled up the bay. Rosie and Jess rode alongside, their stirrups near to touching.

'If we can see *them*, they can see *us*,' Jake said.

'Reckon. That got some meanin'?' Jess asked, thoughtfully.

'Tyler ain't that long out o' trainer pants. So in his predicament, don't

155

you think he'd be out front, yellin' or somethin'? It's what *you* used to do.'

Jess nodded. 'Yeah, I remember,' he said, and immediately yelled across the pasture. 'Tyler. Tyler Galt, you in there?'

There was no response and Jess heeled his horse into a trot. Across the shallow yard, he swung down onto the steps, was fast through the door and into the main room. He saw Tyler and ran forward, his eyes wary and searching the shadows.

'He's livin',' he said, as Rosie and Jake pushed in close behind. 'Bit o' rough housin', nothin' worse.'

Rosie levered a pan of water from the kitchen pump, and almost immediately Tyler was grumping back to life.

'Hah, it's the water he don't like,' Jess ribbed thoughtlessly.

'Where's Tad? Where's Tad?' Rosie was demanding.

Jake stared around him, took notice of Jess who nodded towards Rosie's bed. He saw Galt's body, looked back to Rosie.

'Tyler, come on,' she pleaded. 'Tell me where Tad is. What happened? Tyler . . . Tyler.'

Tyler moved his jaw. 'Aagh. They must've took him. Roach was here . . . must've took him,' he groaned.

'Oh no,' Rosie whispered, sickened.

'Yeah, him an' that detective.' Tyler tried to sit up. 'I told him we knew what he was doin'. He was goin' to wait here for you, Rosie. It was Boone said to take Tad.' Tyler drank some of the water from the pan. 'I couldn't stop 'em, Rosie.'

Jake nodded. 'You weren't expected to. It ain't your fault.'

Rosie looked uncomfortably at Jake, then got to her feet. Angrily she made for the front door, but Jake turned quickly on his good foot and grabbed her arm.

'Gettin' burned up at anythin' *I* say, ain't goin' to get the kid back, Rosie,' he said, letting go of her. 'It's what he wants you to do. You'll be playin' into his hands. Tad's safe enough. We'll get him back, I swear. He represents some years of good livin', for Boone.'

Jess exchanged a sceptical looking glance with his pa. 'Yeah. Gives a new meanin' to livin' high off the hog, don't it?' he suggested.

'Now really ain't the time, Jess. So just shut it,' Jake advised gruffly.

'What do you think we should do?' Rosie asked.

Before Jake could respond, a low, rumbling cough came from the bed. They all stared at each other for a moment, then Jess pulled aside the partly screening curtain, to see Galt's head twisted towards them.

Jake and Rosie mouthed cuss words of shock.

'Somethin' about your pa you forgot to mention?' Jess suggested drily.

'I was goin' to tell you about it,' Tyler said, struggling to his knees. 'It sure looked like he was dyin'.'

A minute later, Rosie was swabbing Galt's sweating, colourless face. The man's pain was evident, but so was his iron will. 'I don't have much of a reason

158

to let you live, Mr Galt. But given the chance, I'm not letting you die, either,' she insisted.

'Not now there's witnesses.' Galt managed to gurgle, before lapsing back into a bitter oblivion.

Rosie got to her feet. 'It's good to be appreciated,' she responded, then tossed the wet cloth onto the rancher's face, and moved back a pace.

'Why'd he say that? He would have known it weren't Rosie shot him,' Tyler said, standing unsteadily. The youngster rubbed his hands across his face. 'He don't want to think it was Roach, does he?'

'Maybe not, Tyler. Maybe he coughed it up for our benefit,' Jake said. 'Seems we all got to considerin' our own forces . . . the enemies within. But that's *his* problem or was. Right now, we got to think ahead. We're obligated to haul the doc out o' Bullhead,' he proposed, then turned to Jess. 'I guess it's down to you, Son.'

'Yeah, it'll be a long rough ride, an'

you don't want to be sharin' a hole in the ground with Galt there,' Jess responded. '*I'm* more obligated in gettin' to Rapid City, so I'll run out the bay.'

Jake nodded reluctantly. It was going to be a hard ride, and he wasn't up to it. There was no waiting for the cover of darkness, either. Rosie's house could be well defended, with the opposition clearly targeted. But without reinforcement from Rapid City, they'd eventually be overwhelmed, most probably all die.

A short while later, Jake shoved a rifle into Jess's saddle boot. 'Keep to the trees for as long as possible, an' don't say nothin' to no one,' Jake warned.

'Yes, you should get by on that,' Rosie accepted. 'If you have to visit the saloon I had to, a grunt should get you understood.'

The two men exchanged a droll glance, and Jess leaped into the saddle. He nudged the bay and within five minutes was clear of Catkin's home pasture.

20

Precious Prospects

Soon after Jess Willem made the shelter of the tree-line, Roach Tolman rode the same trail to the Catkin pasture.

Inside the small ranch house, the three defenders had girded themselves for action. They had a rifle apiece, ammunition brought from Two Jays, and Jake had his .44 Colt.

From a niche in the front door, Jake watched the riders approach the ranch outbuildings. 'Looks like Tolman's on the way in. An' with a fistful o' town help, if I ain't mistaken,' he said calmly. 'Rosie, you an' Tyler keep watch from the back an' south. I'll cover the front, an' hope they don't go circlin' where we can't see 'em.'

'I bet they never even sneezed at Jess's dust,' Tyler speculated, as if reading Jake's mind.

Looking unsure as to what to expect from the house, Tolman halted his men at the yard gate.

Jake realized he'd let them get too close, and fired a warning bullet that clanged noisily into the iron of a nearby plough. He cursed as the bunching horsemen turned and rode off a safe distance, cursed again when Tolman broke away to advance on his own.

He levered another round into the breech, as Tolman walked his horse on through the gate. 'Hold up, Tolman, an' state your business,' he called. 'I'm comin' out.'

'You can't trust him. Stay here, Jake,' Rosie protested.

'I've got to face him, Rosie, an' he knows it. But he also knows ... or thinks he knows what you're capable of. So he can't rate his chances of livin' long if he puts a bullet in me.' With that, Jake pulled back the door, stood on the top step and swung up the barrel of the rifle.

'How's old Hiram?' Tolman immediately mocked.

Jake thought for a second. 'Fine. He's doin' just fine.'

Tolman glared back at him. 'That's good, 'cause it's him I come to talk to, Willem.'

'You'll talk to *me*,' Jake said harshly. 'What have you done with Tad? If you've so much as spat near him . . . '

'He's safe,' Tolman retorted quickly. 'Let me talk to Rosie . . . bring her out.'

'Believe me, that ain't a good idea, Tolman. She can hear you well enough, from where she's got a big fifty pointed right at your vitals.'

Suddenly unsure of himself, Tolman's eyes flicked across the front of the log house. 'You tell her,' he started. 'You tell her, that one way or another, Boone's headed back up the Missouri. An' as far as any one else is concerned, whoever shot Mr Galt, got away . . . no one got to see 'em proper.'

Jake puffed and shook his head.

'Callin' you stupid really is unfair on mules, Tolman. Now, if you don't want to get shot for trespass . . . '

Tolman kicked his horse forward a couple of steps. 'It's *you* that's doin' a big, bad trespass, Willem. You an' your boy. Turn that stallion over to me and you can clear the county with all you can load on that freighter o' yours. Be best if Tyler goes along, but Rosie stays here . . . with the kid.' The HOG foreman wheeled his horse in a tight circle. 'That's a real precious prospect,' he snarled. 'Take it or leave it.'

Jake eased his back against the door. 'I guess we'll have to leave it,' he countered, and lifted the rifle barrel directly at Tolman. 'An' talkin' o' prospects, just how you reckonin' on gettin' beyond the yard gate?'

For a long moment, Tolman sat reckoning on Jake's threat. Then he grinned icily and spurred his horse.

★   ★   ★

Jake shut the door behind him. He'd waited, watched while the men who remained argued. One man stayed just beyond the gate, and two others rode off in different directions. The fourth cantered his horse to the edge of the south pasture.

Tyler and Rosie had been watching Tolman ride away to the south. 'He's goin' back to HOG,' Tyler said.

'Yeah, he knows no harm's goin' to come to him there. The others'll keep us penned in until he gets back,' Jake said calmly. He saw them look at him, felt for their twin resolve and courage. 'From now on, even if you think the air's movin', just hurl lead at it. At least we can make 'em think there's four of us.'

'What's a big fifty, Jake?' Rosie asked.

'The business tool of a buffalo hunter, Rosie. Carries a worse fear than the Devil or God even, when you're starin' at the wrong end. Pity we ain't got one.'

They stood nervy in the silence, alert

to the sound of Hiram Galt's irregular breathing. To Jake, it didn't sound too far off the death rattle. As the minutes passed, he became mindful of the Tolman men who'd rode east and west, and he was right to be.

The first bullet slashed through the shutter that Tyler had eased open, and Jake ducked away from fragments of flying glass. Then, there followed an immediate and calculated fusillade from both flanks. Most of the bullets went into the log walls, a few buried deep in the chinking, some took the window shutters away from their hinges.

A bullet caught a hanging lamp, and showered Tyler's face and neck with oil.

'Get away from the windows,' Jake yelled. Some plates and clay pots were smashed from their shelves in the scullery and Rosie shrieked in discord.

Tyler gave a startled, wide-eyed grin and waved that he was all right. Rosie cried out for what to do.

'Don't know. Just act like a mud fish

while you're doin' it,' Jake yelled, through the pounding crash of bullets.

Rosie made her way over to look at Galt. 'He's all right,' she said. 'He's still breathing and there's no new holes I can see.'

Jake muttered a cynical response and moved over to the window that Rosie was keeping watch from. He knew that one of the men who'd fired would want to check out his handiwork, see the effect of his onslaught shooting.

The man was looking from behind a low stack of chopped logs. To a fair shot he presented a fair target, and Jake sucked air. 'Then there were three,' he said as he drew a bead and squeezed the trigger.

The rifleman took Jake's bullet low in his throat. His head jerked, then his body twisted. He clutched out despairingly as he fell dying, his blood already colouring the logs as they tumbled around him.

His colleague shouted a name, then returned to pumping bullets back at the east-facing side of the house. Jake whirled away from the window, with his back to the wall, motioned for Rosie and Tyler to stay down. After a heavy, but short while he nodded, indicated that now they put back some gunfire.

The three of them then scrambled into position. They poured a torrent of fire across the pasture, gagging as the thick pall of gunsmoke filled their eyes and throats.

Tyler was shaken with excitement. 'We all OK?' he spluttered.

Jake looked over at Rosie and winked. 'Yeah, we're all in one piece, kid. But one o' them sure ain't.'

'I saw someone movin' north,' Tyler continued. 'We can't hit anyone from there.'

'Yeah, reckon the jasper who was out front, thinks the same. Meantime I'll just take a look at your pa, Tyler.' Jake added.

Tyler crawled over to the front of the house, and in similar style Jake moved to the bed. Rosie had pressed some balsam into his chest wound, and it had obviously relieved some of the pain. Jake flinched when he saw Galt staring up at him, but he leaned in close.

'You ain't goin' to miss the show, are you?' Jake said. 'You got much pain?'

'Don't feel a thing. Probably the larkspur I've had poked in me,' Galt rasped ungratefully. 'What the hell's goin' on out there?'

A bullet smacked into the wall above their heads, and Jake ducked, then he smiled grimly. 'Well, we sure ain't bringin' in the sheaves. No, your foreman's taken over, Galt. Some of his men have got us pinned down. So, what do you think they're goin' to do when they get here, eh? Roach Tolman an' his HOG outfit.'

Galt glowered, his body rigid with ineffectual anger. 'What the hell is this stinkin' mess you've plugged me with?' he said. 'You want a slow killin' on that woman's conscience this time?'

'You were almost right first time, Galt. It's wolf poison,' Jake hissed. 'You know it was Tolman shot you. We, all of us here, know it.'

Jake looked around to make sure Rosie and Tyler couldn't hear. He bent in close to Galt's ear. 'But it won't be Rosie doin' you any more harm,' he whispered. 'Because, if my son ain't back with the sheriff before Tolman gets here, *I'll* kill you. I'll call Tolman's men a bunch o' heifer brands. Then, when they retaliate — as they surely will — I'll get you propped up at the nearest window.'

21

Decreasing Numbers

The long rays of sunset were reddening the timber tops when Jake saw the incoming riders. 'What's it they say about misfortune arrivin' on horseback but departin' on foot?' he muttered wryly to himself.

Three . . . four . . . five. He counted uneasily as Tolman and his men swung from west to south. With three of them lying low somewhere between the house and the trees, the one-time HOG foreman had maybe eight men with him now. Jake wondered when Jess would make it back . . . *if* he'd ever make it back, what Rosie and Tyler would make of their chances.

He knew Tolman would be thinking there'd be four rifles defending the house, hoped it would make them more cautious in attack. With only three sides to the house to fire from, their own few guns could appear to be more. With some luck, good shooting, and if the ammunition lasted, so too would they.

'They might try for the back corner,' Jake called to Rosie. 'If they *do*, try an' stop 'em. But my guess is they're stretchin' our thoughts. They're goin' to regroup an' challenge us head on. Tyler, how you fixed?'

'I'll stay with the lookin' out . . . point my gun where there's no danger. You can get on with the battle.' The frustration was clear in Tyler's voice as he shouted back.

Jake shook his head, considered a target as Tolman and his men galloped at the front of Rosie's house. He swore, cursed one and all, and started firing.

But the riders spread out and Jake was restricted in movement, couldn't get much accuracy with his shooting. He clenched his jaw with deliberation then he swore again, shouted for Jess to hurry up as the acrid smoke crowded his face.

A HOG man dropped from his saddle. He tried to get to his feet, even managed a futile grab for the tail of his horse before collapsing.

'Tough luck, feller,' Jake muttered, his rifle smouldering in his hands. He was bleeding from his forehead where a flying splinter had slashed him.

Three of the riders attempted to avoid Jake's startling barrage of fire, and Rosie and Tyler got the opportunity to open up from their side wall positions.

'He's hit,' Tyler yelled almost immediately. 'Ain't seen him before . . . must've signed up from town.'

'Who taught you how to shoot?' Jake asked.

'It was Roach,' Tyler said.

But Jake had guessed the answer. He was already twisting a grin at the irony, as he slumped down with his back against the wall. 'An' then they were six,' he persisted with his deathly musing as he thumbed more cartridges into the rifle's magazine. 'What would we do without family, eh Rosie?' he then said enigmatically after a more thoughtful moment. He put the gun aside and fumbled for the makings of a cigarette. 'Can you see what's goin' on out there?' he asked.

'Tolman's just lost another two men, that's what's going on,' Rosie replied. 'Now there's a horse running for the trees . . . I think they're rounding on the front again, Jake. There's someone . . . oh no . . . he's . . . '

'Rosie. What's wrong?' Tyler yelled, thinking she'd been hit.

Jake threw himself forward onto his elbows. 'Rosie . . . Rosie . . . '

'I'm all right. One of those men . . . he was trying to get . . . he was . . . ' Rosie stuttered.

'What man? What about him?' Jake got to his feet, looked to where Rosie had pointed. He saw a man crawling towards the shelter of the irrigation ditch that ran to and from the run-around stream. 'He don't look like no ranch hand. I reckon Tyler just shot your Mitchell detective, Rosie.'

Tyler shook his head, opened his mouth to say something when Rosie spoke up. 'That's Derram Kale . . . Tad's father,' she said, breathless and taut with shock.

In the abrupt silence that followed, Jake stopped himself from wondering if Rosie really was a killer. 'I'm tryin' to figure out if this is good or bad, Rosie,' he said, as the alternative to asking. 'Help me out.'

'It's surely good, Jake. It means it's Derram who's trailed me here.' Rosie's voice carried a trace of excitement. 'There's no one called Henry Boone from Mitchell, or anywhere else. If he's lied to Tolman, why not about the murder charge?'

Jake looked at Tyler who was clearly trying to make sense of the latest revelation. 'Yeah,' he said. 'I suppose it would hold water as long as he didn't run into anyone who knew him.' He got to his feet to look from the window. Fifty yards away from the house, Kale had dragged himself from the ditch, but now he lay still.

'Is Bench's old pie buggy still out back?' Jake asked.

'Yes, it's still there,' Rosie said.

'An' your little pony?'

'Yes. In the lean-to with Tyler's roan. Why?'

'If Kale's still alive, he can tell one of us where his kid . . . your nephew is.'

Rosie had her doubts about Jake's ability to make it, but couldn't dispute his proposal. 'What makes you think he'll oblige?' she asked.

'Right now, I'm in a lot better shape than he is, so he'll oblige. I was hopin' Jess would be here by now. He could try to stop me,' Jake confessed, with a rueful smile. 'Still, them out there won't be expectin' much from me in the way of heroics. I should be with Kale before they realize what's happenin'.'

'You'll get there in one piece. And it's not you being with *him*, that worries me,' Rosie reasoned. 'It's not being with us.'

'Yeah,' Tyler agreed.

Jake looked at them both. 'That's often the way,' he said. 'But I'm comin' back. Nonetheless, if you reckon I'm in trouble, you start shootin'. Use all the ammunition if you have to, then throw things.'

Jake made himself spare as he eased through the back door. He made his luck, got partly screened from the south by the north-east corner of the house.

22

The Hearing

After quickly hitching up Rosie's tough little pony, he swerved the buggy west, keeping the house between him and Tolman's riders. He'd almost made up the ground when he heard the yelling.

Three of the riders raced across the pasture to bring him within range of their rifles. But from the house, Rosie and Tyler were ready and laid down heavy fire in an effort to hold them back.

When Jake reached Kale, he swung the side of the buggy against the north end of the pasture. The man wasn't dead and Jake managed to prop his body against the front wheel. Then he stepped awkwardly up to the footboard and dragged Kale on to the benched seat.

As the bullets ripped chaotically into the buggy's quarters, Jake grinned anxiously at the concerted effort to stop him. Going with Tolman's current thinking, if Rosie had decided to stay and make a fight, the man known as Henry Boone was a dud round.

Jake yelled and jerked the lines for the pony to run wildly back to the rear of the house. Tyler was waiting expectantly and he helped drag the slumped body through the shattered crocks on the floor of the scullery.

Rosie was covering them as well as she could from the east and south sides. 'Are you all right, Jake?' she shouted.

'Yeah, o' course. But this feller ain't too lively, Rosie. Keep an eye on him all the same. If he's who you say he is, he's still marriage kin.'

'It's gone quiet,' Rosie said, as she moved away from a window. 'You don't think they're about to surrender?'

'Yeah, an' I'm the Hamfat Man.'

Rosie shrugged and took a step

forward, looked down at Jake's foot.

'Some o' the bones are still workin',' he assured her, as he stamped his heel on the floor a couple of times. 'Kale's the one who ain't too bonny. When he talks though, I want him heard. Galt still makin' noises?'

'Yes. Just now he told Tyler the fight wasn't good judgement.'

'Hah,' Jake snorted. 'On whose part? He's been thinkin' about what I'd do to him if Jess didn't get here.'

With one hand gripping the back of Kale's collar, Jake dragged the man close to where Galt was lying. Then he stepped back a pace.

Kale's eyes opened when Rosie kneeled close to the bedside. It was as if he knew she was there. 'Hello, Martha. Couldn't remember whether it was your hair or your heart was black,' he said, painfully.

'What are you doing here, Derram? Why can't you leave us be?' she asked despondently. 'You don't really want Tad, we both know that.'

Jake moved forward. 'Where you hurtin'?' he intercepted harshly.

'All over. I'm hurtin' real bad all over,' Kale told him.

Jake nodded once. 'That's good,' he said, 'because all over's where I'm goin' to kick you if you don't tell us the truth about what happened. Now talk!'

The threat brought Kale around for a few more minutes. Jake, edging closer, intimidated him into telling what had happened after the shooting in Pickstown.

Kale told them he'd convinced the law in Mitchell that he'd had a bit of a mishap. He'd been toying with Rosie's pocket pistol in her hotel room and shot himself. 'I told 'em the small gun was an unusual one . . . that I was showing the kid.'

Kale claimed that Rosie had panicked and went on the run. Because of Tad she'd been frightened, didn't want to get charged with a default murder with *him* to look after. 'The law weren't convinced, I'll give 'em that,' he said.

'But there was no other witness or evidence, so they lost interest, and brought no charge. It weren't long before I was Henry Boone and set out to trail her. People give directions more easy when it's a kid you're lookin' for.'

Kale was sweating with the pain of talking, but he closed his eyes and carried on. 'I found out what that pig Tolman wanted. I had to decide . . . '

Jake hoped that it wasn't true about a falling man being pushed too hard. 'Tell us where Tad is,' he demanded, before Kale could explain anything more away.

Kale's eyes opened, swivelled to find Rosie. 'Woodend . . . he's there,' he stuttered. His eyes turned misty and closed again. 'Ain't fared too well in front o' guns. It woulda been Tolman this time . . . same as he did for Galt.' The Missouri River postman smiled despairingly. 'Who the hell's to be trusted?' he groaned.

Rosie turned away, watched Jake lift the blanket from Galt to cover Kale. The rancher's eyes were closed, but he was playing possum, had heard Kale's last few words.

'I've met nicer fellers,' he said, pulling Rosie to her feet. 'Least you don't have to make up any more stories about his death.'

Rosie's blush rose slowly from the neck. 'I can't believe I told you those things,' she said.

'They were more for you to believe, not me,' Jake suggested selflessly. 'Anythin' will do when in need. Ain't that so, Tyler?'

'Yeah,' Tyler said, once again not fully understanding. 'An' we know Tad's safe.'

Jake thought for a second. 'So, where the hell's this Woodend place?' he asked.

'It's Woody. Curly Woodend's the old HOG wrangler,' Tyler explained. 'That's who Tad's with . . . where they took him. Jeez, Tad'll be cuttin' cow critters, by the time we get to him.'

'That's useful,' Jake ribbed, winked reassuringly at Rosie. Then he swore violently and edged alongside the west-facing side window. 'They're scatterin'. I think they're gettin' ready to hit us again . . . what's left of 'em.'

'Where they goin'?' Tyler wanted to know.

'North . . . our blind side. Let's get some dust on our bellies.'

'You sure have a way with words, Jake,' Rosie said, the emotion and stress cracking her voice. 'Why not something to make us feel better?'

'I think I can hear Jess comin',' he offered.

23

Hanging On

The occupants of the Catkin ranch house had no need of night lamps. The hunter's moon came to their aid. The surrounding pasture was turned to blue day, made less of Tolman's menace.

'No hooties on the wing tonight. Even the fireflies ain't botherin' to light up,' Tyler said.

'Just keep your head down,' Jake charged. 'If Tolman does decide to bother us, at least we can hold 'em off while the shells last,' he added.

'That won't be long, Jake,' Rosie said. 'There's about a handful apiece.'

'I know, I'm sorry. I brought over all we had. Out at Two Jays we looked to dealin' in beef an' beans . . . not bullets.'

Jake immediately regretted sounding

as though he was resentful at fighting Rosie's corner, and he wasn't. 'I didn't mean that the way it sounds,' he added hastily.

'I know you didn't,' Rosie responded just as quickly.

'Don't reckon I've ever spent so much time bein' of an apologetic nature,' Jake reflected. 'It's kind o' hard to get used to.'

'You'll find out what bein' sorry means when Roach decides to do what's right,' came the voice from behind them. Though Hiram Galt's voice was weak, it still resonated with an edge of combat.

Jake snorted derisively. 'There's stuff livin' in creek holes that know more about what's right, than Roach Tolman,' he rasped. 'Goddamn you, Galt. We're fightin' to keep us *all* alive. Do you believe Tolman's ever lettin' you give orders again?' Jake shook his head. 'No. Your not-so-trusty foreman's out to finish the job he started. You heard what Kale said.'

'Yeah, I heard what he said . . . who-ever he was,' Galt came back. 'But there's some things don't change in a man. For some reason, Roach's wits are caught in a storm. He'll pull through.'

Tyler looked over at his father. 'You're wrong, Pa, an' you sayin' them things don't make 'em right,' he said unhappily. 'The sheriff's comin' with Jess, an' when he gets here, you'll see.'

★   ★   ★

In the early morning, a rider emerged from the trees on the eastern side of the pasture. The man turned south and Jake noticed the extra horse he was leading. His body was gripped with cold, his heart thumped and he hardly took a breath as the first daylight rippled on the withers of his bay. The stallion was being led by Fole Stiller.

Jake balled his fist into the wall. 'Oh no,' he said thickly, as the bitterness filled him. But he fought to regain his composure, keep control of his emotions until he had a contingency plan. It wouldn't serve any purpose to let them know what he'd seen. He also knew that whatever it was had happened to Jess, within moments from now, Tolman and his men would know there was only three of them in the house, including young Tyler.

'What's up, Jake? Do you think they're going to rush us again?' Rosie asked with chance timing.

'Oh yeah, they'll rush us. As sure as that sun's comin' up.'

'I'm sorry, Jake . . . sorry, Tyler,' Rosie said, near to despair. 'It is only because of me, that you're here . . . in this . . . this dreadful chaos.'

'Yeah, I can see how it looks, Rosie, but it really ain't the *only* reason . . . not any more,' Jake replied.

Tolman was down a few men, wasn't going to take being kept at bay by *anyone* too lightly. The fact that it was Jake again, but with backing from Rosie and Tyler would make him easy on the trigger, angry enough to make a deciding assault.

Jake lifted out the locking brace, dropped the latch and pressed his knee against the front door until it opened an inch or two. He knew they'd be coming from the north-west corner, and he placed Tyler at the window alongside him. Rosie took the west-facing window.

When Tolman and his men rode in, there was no time for the defenders to pick targets, use any sort of effective aim. They fired indiscriminately, reckless in their use of ammunition.

Tyler was right, and Jake recognized one or two 'punchers, broke drifters from Bullhead who swarmed into the yard. With deafening mayhem, they scattered Rosie's chickens from their coop, and a half-wild cat from its stealthy advance through the kitchen garden.

Jake kicked the door to, threw down his empty rifle and grabbed his Colt. He'd seen horsemen approaching, and fast. They were at a distance though, still on the far side of the wagon road. 'Hold your fire,' he shouted. 'There's somethin' you should know . . . that we should talk about.'

'We *do* know, an' talkin' won't help. We're out of ammunition . . . firin' dry,' Tyler said.

Jake took a short, sharp look at Tyler. There was a new force to the youngster's voice, the hair didn't seem quite so curly any more, the build, stronger set. Then he shook his head against the ongoing noise from outside. 'No, it ain't that,' he mumbled, thumbing the cylinder of his gun. 'Could be worse.'

He thought they were going to be with him, pick up on the concern. But Rosie was staring and pointing across the room, had found something else to shock her. Jake pulled back the hammer of the Colt and dropped to his knees, brought the gun to bear on Hiram Galt.

Galt was up and standing beside the bed. The three of them watched, captivated, as the badly wounded man grabbed at a high-back chair and took a step forward. It was a feat of staggering resolve for him to stand, let alone walk, the stamp of a man who still wanted control of people around him.

Jake swung away, took a step back when boots stomped onto the short run of steps. He moved to one side as the door crashed open, but his eyes remained fixed on the rugged figure in front of him.

The weathered features of Galt's face were now doughy and sweated with pain. That, the gory tattered clothing, and the wad of bloody bandages, stopped Roach Tolman dead in his tracks as he came through the door.

Tolman mouthed a silent, disbelieving oath as he attempted to push himself back to the cover of two men who'd followed him in.

Galt's voice cut through the room. 'We been expectin' you, Roach. Willem here seems to think you've come to finish me off. Seems to think it's *you* givin' HOG's orders now.' The rancher steadied himself and his eyes suddenly set hard. 'Not even when I'm dead, you cowardly, murderin' scum,' he rasped with a bone-chilling smile.

Addressing himself to Rosie, it was Galt's voice again that broke the ensuing, hushed stand-off. 'I've spent most o' my many years thinkin' I'm right. Comes in handy for a man who don't take to bein' wrong. It never stopped me from knowin' an' seein' though, despite what young Tyler thinks.'

Tyler had his eyes fixed on Rosie. It was his way of hedging his emotions as his father continued.

'Roach was shovin' you people around, even as you shook off your travellin' dust . . . doin' it in my name, too. But then he gunned down poor old Tom . . . ordered Stiller to ambush Willem.' Galt gave an almost imperceptible nod to Rosie. 'When I said I knew most things that went on, I meant it,' he said meaningfully. Then the man's gaze wavered as he turned inevitably to Tyler.

'I have been wrong before, Son ... done some bad things, too. But I only ever told Roach to keep an eye on 'em. Difference is, I always knew when to stop ... like now ... he don't. So you got to get your new-found friends to clip his horns ... before ... '

Galt's life was flowing from him, and his legs buckled. Jake and Tyler stepped in and supported him, eased him to the floor.

For the two HOG punchers who stood behind Tolman, there'd only ever been one boss. They'd just forgotten for a while, needed something to remind them. As Galt went down they moved, but Tolman was further on. He pulled the shiny plated Colt with his left hand, thrust the rifle barrel with his right. 'Remember, dead men don't do anything ever again ... ever,' he threatened.

As Tolman forced his way out to the steps, Rosie and Tyler heeded Jake's warning to stay quiet. Jake had to play for time. Their ammunition was nearly gone, and he wanted to check out the repositioning of the HOG men, where Fole Stiller was, what he and Tolman would do next. When Jake exchanged his Colt for the Winchester, Tyler looked gloomy. He wasn't sure of the number of remaining bullets.

24

Broken Bonds

Most of the men who'd been hired by Tolman realized they'd been hood-winked. For a dollar-a-day 'puncher, gunfighting made for a bleak future. Out in the Catkin yard, their involvement ended with the retribution of threats, curses and a clumsy struggle. Not one of them was actually looking out for Tolman and Stiller. But Jake was. 'Hey, General,' he called out to Tyler. 'I'm takin' the fight to them . . . 'cause I'm owed it.' Then he gritted his teeth and shouting for his back to be covered, he made an awkward but confident shift to the fighting ground. Almost immediately he had to parry a fist. He swung the rifle viciously, while trying to see where Tolman had gone. He wondered most about Stiller, though — a man with more than one reason why he'd want to settle up with Jess.

Like Galt, Jake wasn't a killer, not a natural one anyway. But now, standing alone, things were different. Stiller might turn away, but Tolman had come too far.

He looked towards the gate that led from the yard to the pasture, felt the stab of pain that returned to grip his right foot. He was wrong about Stiller. As the man walked towards him, he cursed, kept his eyes straight ahead when the bullet smashed high into his left shoulder.

'Ain't the work for bushwhackin' yellow bellies,' Jake called, as the first shot from his Winchester chewed out the left side of Stiller's neck. For a moment, Jake saw the raw flesh before the gush of bright blood. For a moment Stiller stayed on his feet. Then he stumbled, made a single scratchy cough, before pulling at his neck scarf. As he buckled to his knees, Jake shot him again. 'That's for my boy, Jess,' he snarled, as he put a bullet as near as he could to the same spot. This time it lifted Stiller up and over onto his back, his blood staining the hard-packed dirt. 'No more kowtowin' to Tolman either,' Jake advised with pitiless sentiment.

'Look out!' Tyler shouted, and Jake swung round just as someone appeared from the back corner of the house. It was Tolman, and he'd brought a shotgun that he was grasping in his white-knuckled hands. Jake continued his movement, but doubled up his left leg, fell forward to drop below the elevation of the twin barrels. He heard one great blast of sound, felt the pulse of air, as a half-ounce of shot sizzled above him. He hit the ground, and with his body still jarring from the shock, brought up the Winchester.

Jake's shot went low, and Tolman gasped as the bullet bored deep, grunted out noisy air at the tearing of his vitals.

'With a little somethin' from Meg

Owers,' Jake bitterly continued his lethal share out.

Tolman caught his legs on a mudsill, over-balanced and fell back against a corner post. But despite his hideous wounds, he managed to retain his grip on the shotgun. As Jake regained his footing and got to his feet, Tolman jerked his finger against the second trigger. The wavering shotgun roared again, and Jake felt the kick, then the warm blood below his right knee.

He swore, shouted 'Not my goddamn leg again,' and swung the Winchester in a short curve. Once again he aimed at Tolman's head and pulled the trigger. He didn't move when the hammer fell against an empty chamber, just stood his ground for the short time it took the man to crumple down dead.

'I was hopin' to kick you to death,' Jake rumbled. Then he turned towards the front door of the house where Tyler and Rosie were standing. With a tired smile, he looked down at his bleeding leg and dropped the empty rifle.

Then he wondered what Rosie was suddenly pointing at, remembered the riders he'd assumed were coming to finish off what Tolman and his men had started.

★ ★ ★

The silver star that was pinned to the first man into the yard, flashed under the rising sun. But it wasn't the badge of the Rapid City sheriff that stirred Jake up; it was the spare, stubbled faces, the slouch hats and dusty garb of the men following.

'It's my goddamn herd,' rasped Jake, eying the group of 'punchers who'd driven his mixed stock up from the North Platte.

One of them walked his cow pony forward slowly. He was slumped in the saddle and the brim of his hat was pulled low. He was dirty, and one of his hands was bandaged. 'Bet you thought I was kickin' up cactus somewhere,' Jess said.

'Christ, Jess, we all thought that,' Jake shouted, laughed as he dragged himself forward. He reached for the reins as Jess swung down. 'Where the hell you been?'

'He never got beyond the nearest town,' drawled the herd boss who'd ambled up. 'Your boy got to playin' tag with a back-shoot specialist.'

'Yeah, that'll be Fole Stiller,' Jake said. 'He's the one who led the stallion back.'

'Yeah,' Jess agreed. 'You forgot to warn me about him. He shot at me an' I dived. That's how I hurt my hand. It weren't that bad, but I lost the horse to him. I thought I could make Bullhead on foot . . . the HOG even. I musta passed out somewhere along the timberline. Next thing I know, it's daybreak an' there's cattle lowin'. The first person I see from the trees is the sheriff. He's alongside Duffy, ridin' swing on our herd.'

Jake looked at the ramrod who offered his hand. 'Duffy Birch,' he said.

'We'd made it to Hot Springs . . . were bedded down,' he explained. 'Sheriff learned we were headin' up east for the basin . . . rode out to look us over. When he finds out who we are an' where we're headed, he says he'll tag along.' Birch grimaced and sputtered a thin stream of tobacco juice. 'When we heard Jess's story, we put the herd into a run. They're no more than an hour behind, an' sheddin' lard. But the boys don't like to miss a fight, Mr Willem. It's their trail-end fun.'

Jake looked at the sheriff. 'How come you were close enough to meet?' he asked. 'It's a big country, an' a ways from Rapid City.'

'I was makin' a circuit trip . . . callin' in at HOG. Wanted to see Galt about a couple of unconnected matters. Timin' was pure serendipity, I guess.'

'Yeah,' Jake said. 'That's always somethin' that's goin' to come along.' Then he looked around him. 'As for the fight, you're all too late. The boys can ride into Bullhead . . . shoot up the

White Glass Saloon,' he recommended. 'That'll be fun . . . an' likely no one'll notice.'

Jess laughed. 'An' keep a look out for the bay. He might just be on the road back to Two Jays.' He flexed the fingers of his bandaged hand, looked towards the body of Stiller, then Tolman. 'Sure are an ugly couple o' birds. I wish I'd been here, Pa,' he said and looked heartfelt about it. 'Looks like Tolman's the one joinin' them canker worms he was tellin' us about. Perhaps some o' the boys can clear Rosie's yard for her.'

Jake nodded, began to say something, but stopped when the sheriff came out of the house. The lawman stepped down into the yard, walked over to Jake and spoke quietly.

'Galt's just died. He didn't want to, but there was nothin' more could be done for him an' he knew it. He told me what's been happenin' here. Enough to make an end of it . . . for me to ride on.'

Jake and Jess looked at each other.

'Not quite, Sheriff,' Jake said. 'An' Jess ain't quite finished, either. If you'd ride with him an' Rosie out to the HOG, you'll find this young Tad feller. Bring him home safe, an' maybe *then* we can all sleep easy.'

'You folks have had trouble enough. But now it's mostly over, do you reckon we got time for a comfort stop . . . stretch our legs? Maybe the lady could fix some coffee . . . some slakin' juice, even,' the sheriff suggested.

Jake gave a quizzical look towards Tyler who was still grinning at Jess having returned safely. 'Yeah, I got just the thing,' he said. 'An' accordin' to Tyler, Tad's probably happy enough bulldoggin' HOG steers for a while longer.'

Rosie moved towards Jake as the others went to the water trough outside of the barn. 'I've got plenty coffee, but I haven't got any 'slakin' juice' . . . not what *he* means, anyway,' she said quietly.

'I know. But *I* have. Edson gave me a

couple o' bottles from his private stock,' he said with a wily wink. 'Let's hope they ain't smashed up.'

The two of them watched a massive Birch cowboy dragging the bodies of Tolman and Stiller into a shed. Two more were lifting Kale down the cabin steps.

'One way to fill outbuildin's,' Jake muttered.

Rosie was unmoved by the quip. 'Are you all right, Jake?' she asked. 'I don't suppose all these wounds mean much to a man who so easily gives up beans for bullets, do they?'

'I'm not hurtin' much, Rosie. Not that you can see. An' I haven't given up on anythin', either. Make o' that what you will.'

'And there was I, thinking you were too old for me,' she said, sounding mischievous.

'Was thinkin'?' Jake queried after a moment's hesitation. 'Somethin's changed?'

'Yes. Since arriving in Bullhead, I've aged about twenty years. Makes us a match, wouldn't you say?' She then smiled warmly.

It was the second time Jake had experienced the feeling. Only this time, he knew he wasn't going to lose out by liking her.

Jess had been watching, was needing a better fix on the state of affairs, and he'd walked up close.

'When my leg an' foot an' shoulder an' head ain't playin' up so much,' Jake said, 'I'm thinkin' o' cuttin' down the timber between here an' Two Jays . . . runnin' the spreads together. I'm also gettin' married. What do you say to that, Jess?'

'I'd say it's a real fine idea, Pa. But I'll be missin' the weddin'. I'm ridin' back to the North Platte with Duffy. Get *me* some excitement.'

Jake and Rosie looked at each other and Jake shrugged. Laughing again, Jess strolled off for his splash in the trough.

'Well, what do you make of that?' Rosie said, her surprise obvious.

'The pup's been carryin' a bone for

you, himself. *That*'s what I make of it. Maybe he needs to stay away until he's dropped it.'

Rosie thought she'd better go and start boiling up the coffee for the men. 'I wouldn't feel so . . . so thrown, if I'd had even the slightest notion,' she said, in the sureness of her feelings for Jake. 'He certainly never let me know how he felt.'

'Yeah, me neither. Shows he got some sense,' Jake responded drily. 'Given time, everythin's sure to get sorted out.'

'I know,' Rosie said. 'What's going to happen at HOG?' she asked.

'It's Tyler's now,' Jake said. 'He can run it with that Curly Woodend feller. That's an outfit that shouldn't have the old man turnin' in his grave.'

'Hmm. And if Jess is hurt, if he really does leave, it'll mean we're on our own.'

'Yeah. But *we're* all grown up.'

We do hope that you have enjoyed reading this large print book.

Did you know that all of our titles are available for purchase?

We publish a wide range of high quality large print books including:
Romances, Mysteries, Classics
General Fiction
Non Fiction and Westerns

Special interest titles available in large print are:
The Little Oxford Dictionary
Music Book, Song Book
Hymn Book, Service Book

Also available from us courtesy of Oxford University Press:
Young Readers' Dictionary
(large print edition)
Young Readers' Thesaurus
(large print edition)

For further information or a free brochure, please contact us at:
Ulverscroft Large Print Books Ltd.,
The Green, Bradgate Road, Anstey,
Leicester, LE7 7FU, England.
Tel: (00 44) **0116 236 4325**
Fax: (00 44) **0116 234 0205**

WEST OF EDEN

Mike Stall

Marshal Jack Adams was tired of people shooting at him. So when the kid came into town sporting a two-gun rig and out to make his reputation — at Adams' expense — it was time to turn in his star and buy that horse ranch he'd dreamed about in the Eden Valley. It looked peaceful, but the valley was on the verge of a range-war and there was only one man to stop it. So Adams pinned on a star again and started shooting back — with a vengeance!

BAR 10 GUNSMOKE

Boyd Cassidy

As always, Bar 10 rancher Gene Adams responded to a plea for help, taking Johnny Puma and Tomahawk. They headed into Mexico to help their friend Don Miguel Garcia. But they were walking into a trap laid by the outlaw known as Lucifer. When the Bar 10 riders arrived at Garcia's ranch, Johnny was cut down in a hail of bullets. Adams and Tomahawk thunder into action to take on Lucifer and his gang. But will they survive the outlaws' hot lead?

THE FRONTIERSMEN

Elliot Conway

Major Philip Gaunt and his former
batman, Naik Alif Khan, veterans of
dozens of skirmishes on British
India's north-west frontier, are fighting the wild and dangerous land of
northern Mexico. Aided by 'Buck-
skin' Carlson, a newly reformed
drunk, they are hunting down
Mexican bandidos who murdered
the major's sister. But it proves to be
a dangerous trail. Death by knife
and gun is never far away. Will they
finally deliver cold justice to the
bandidos?